CURSE OF THE WOLF

MAGNETIC MAGIC
BOOK 5

LINDSAY BUROKER

1

THE SWORD SLASHED TOWARD MY HEAD WITH STARTLING SPEED. I jerked my practice blade up, barely in time to block it. Frustrated at being caught off guard, I threw more muscle into the effort than necessary and had to hurry to return my weapon to a defensive posture in front of my body.

My green-haired, twenty-year-old instructor never used more effort than necessary and usually whipped his blade back in time to punish me for overextending myself. This time, Yuto merely cocked an eyebrow and stepped back, waving that we could take a break.

Thank the moon. I only resisted baring my teeth—especially the extra sharp canines granted to me by my werewolf heritage—because I was too busy panting.

"You are very strong for a..." Yuto waved his practice sword vaguely around the empty dojo, as if the rest of the sentence might be found floating with the dust motes in the sun beaming through the front windows.

"A woman?"

"An older woman."

I scowled at him. "I'm forty-five. That's middle-aged, not *older*."

Nobly, I fought down the urge to rush to the bathroom and peer at my hairline in the mirror. With everything going on in my life of late, it had been a while since I'd spent quality time with a bottle of raven-black dye.

"When I visited your apartment complex, I met your son," Yuto said blandly. "We are almost the same age."

"So? Your mom is middle-aged too. Not *older*. I promise you."

He cocked his head as he regarded me. "Actually, you are quite strong for a woman of any age. And for many men."

"My job involves a lot of heavy lifting." I didn't know if Yuto, or his uncle who owned the dojo we were practicing in, believed in werewolves or other paranormal beings, but most people didn't.

"Aren't you the property manager?"

"I do a lot of the repairs myself. Including junk removal when tenants move out without taking everything with them, like their crappy couch stained by beer and cat puke." Just that morning, I'd hauled *that* beauty out of a recently vacated apartment. My life continued to be glamorous.

"That must be it." Another eyebrow cock accompanied the words.

If Yuto intended to question me further, I didn't find out, because he was distracted by whistling that floated through an open window overlooking the parking lot.

Outside, the Christmas snow had melted, with a string of pleasant fifty-degree days following, so Duncan had the perfect weather for metal detecting. He waved his device back and forth, examining the parking lot and landscaping around it in the search for who knew what treasures.

The whistling paused, and a faint beeping wafted in, though I knew without a doubt that the pavement out there didn't hold any great prizes. Duncan hadn't said so, but he had come along to keep an eye on me, and he would toss aside the metal detector and leap to my defense if some of Radomir's thugs showed up. Not long ago, we'd again thwarted the old man's plans, and he wouldn't forget.

As if to deny my certainty that there were no treasures, Duncan one-handedly hefted a wooden bench with cement supports to swing his device under it. Something had caught his eye.

"He is also quite strong," Yuto mused.

"He removes a lot of junk too."

"He said he was a traveling treasure hunter, not a property manager."

"Traveling *junk* hunter, maybe."

After witnessing Duncan pulling not one but two priceless magical medallions up from bodies of water, I supposed I should tease him less about the quality of treasures he found. But... maybe not. The evening before, he'd taken me on a date to the Ballard Marina and used his super-strong magnets to pull out three broken bicycles, two rusty car fenders, and a dog crate with kelp woven through the metal bars. Treasures, they had not been.

A *thunk* sounded as Duncan released the bench and moved to investigate a stormwater grate. The excited, "Oooh," as the beeps intensified made me glad he hadn't taken me to a wastewater treatment plant for our date.

Yuto waved for me to lift my practice sword. Was the break already over?

I must have made a sour face—perhaps displaying those canines again—because he offered, "You're progressing well and have excellent reflexes. We could move from wooden swords to the blade you wish to learn to use to... poke werewolves."

When we'd met, I'd asked how long it would take me to master such a skill. He must have thought it a joke, but who knew what he knew?

Other than that busy single eyebrow of his, Yuto wasn't that expressive of a kid, so I could rarely guess what he was thinking.

Not like my eighteen-year old son, Austin, who was usually easy to read. Though I'd had a hard time telling what *he* was thinking the last couple of days he'd been home for Christmas vacation. He'd been calm and collected during the battle the night that Duncan and I—and my niece Jasmine and intern Bolin—had rescued Austin from kidnappers, but he'd also, for the first time in his life, seen me change into a werewolf. Before, I'd always hidden that part of my heritage from Austin and his brother, Cameron. I'd wanted to explain my reasons to Austin, but... he'd pointedly not asked. He'd avoided speaking about anything of consequence and hurried off to the airport the day before, returning to his Air Force training.

I had no idea when I would see Austin again and couldn't help but be disappointed. And sad. My other son barely spoke to me. Austin had been more understanding after the divorce. I would hate to lose my relationship with him.

"Ms. Valens?" Yuto prompted at my silence.

"Sorry. Yes. I *do* long to put the pointy end of that sword into werewolves, but it's been misplaced."

It had been *stolen* by a bunch of local thugs who had turned vandalizing Sylvan Serenity's parking lot into a hobby.

"Misplaced," Yuto mouthed.

"*Temporarily* misplaced." Duncan, now standing in the doorway, nodded firmly at me.

"Yes," I said, hoping that would prove true.

He'd given the sword to me as a gift, and it had silver and magic melded into the blade, making it not only invaluable because it was a centuries-old artifact but because it could wound werewolves. Thanks to our powerful regenerative abilities, our kind tended to be hard to kill.

"How go the lessons, my lady?" Duncan acknowledged Yuto with a cheerful wave, then smiled and bowed toward me, managing to hold the metal detector out wide without clunking the door frame.

"I'm progressing, I'm told."

Yuto nodded. "She is athletic and a pleasure to teach."

This time, *my* eyebrow journeyed upward. "You just called me old."

"*Older.*"

"I assumed you thought I would need a cane to leave the premises."

"Only if you're stiff and sore after exercise."

No, I usually wasn't, not since I'd stopped taking the sublimation potion that had dampened my werewolf magic for more than twenty years of my life. Even if my existence had turned chaotic since then, I did appreciate the perks the power conveyed. I'd also been sleeping better and had more energy, a good thing since I'd needed it to fight cranky family members and megalomaniacal bad guys.

"Perhaps *we* could spar for a bit?" Duncan pointed to me, touched his own chest, then waved toward wooden practice swords leaning against a wall. "It might be invigorating, and it's good for your training to battle other types of opponents."

"You know how to fight with a sword?" I asked.

"Of *course*, my lady. A gentleman always learns how to duel."

"A gentleman from 1703, maybe."

"I'm not quite that old."

I eyed his short salt-and-pepper hair. It was thick and lush, but *he* didn't bother applying dye to hide the grays.

"I'll be happy to demonstrate my youthful fitness." Duncan plucked up one of the practice swords.

Yuto stepped back, pulling out his phone to look at the time. "There is a class in a half hour. You can have the floor until the little kids start showing up."

When Duncan put aside his metal detector and removed his

shirt, my gaze snagged on his muscular torso. His assurances of his youthful fitness were not unfounded. The wolf-headed medallion he'd recently found, the match for the one my mom owned, lay nestled in the valley between his pectorals, drawing attention to the rounded muscles.

My eyes lingered longer than I intended, and Duncan turned to face me before I looked away. Had he caught me ogling him?

"You think you need to be shirtless to spar with me?" I asked.

"The better to distract my opponents, especially my *female* opponents." He winked.

Damn, he *had* caught me ogling him.

"Do you get a lot of women lunging at you with swords, wanting to duel?"

"Not copious numbers, no. When women lunge at me, they usually have other things on their minds."

"Feeling full of yourself today, are you?" I raised my practice sword, nodding that I was ready, though I hadn't done a lot of free sparring yet and didn't know what to expect. The majority of my lessons had involved repeating different parries and combinations of attacks over and over.

"It's probably the medallion." Duncan touched the gold chain hanging around his neck. Though it was a family heirloom from my pack, he'd been the one to locate it after it had been lost for generations, so my mother had agreed to let him borrow it. She'd even implied that he was invited to join our pack and wear it permanently, but the itinerant Duncan hadn't given any indication that he wanted that. He was helping me with my problems, but who knew how long he would stay in the area? Seattle couldn't have *that* many fantastic treasures in its lakes and in Puget Sound.

Sadness, especially the anticipation of loneliness, crept into me as I imagined Duncan leaving. With my sons gone, it was hard not to feel like everyone in my life was abandoning me. Further, with Sylvan Serenity up for sale, I was on the verge of losing my home and my job of more than two decades too.

"I'd intended to try to poke you with this sword," Duncan said, his practice blade raised, "but you look so glum that it would be like beating a puppy."

"At least you didn't compare me to a granny with a cane." I shot Yuto a dark look, but he was engrossed in looking for dates on a phone app and didn't acknowledge the comment. Shaking away my gloomy thoughts, I dropped into a fighting stance. "Come at me, big boy."

"Hah." Duncan swung toward my head, slowly enough that I not only had time to parry but employed the correct technique in doing so.

He nodded, swinging again, and I realized he was merely helping me train. This wouldn't involve a sound thumping. Or so I thought. Once Duncan determined that I could parry the easy blows, he picked up his speed and started throwing in two- and three-move combinations.

I concentrated, wanting to show the person who'd paid for my lessons that he hadn't wasted his money. Once we got that sword back, I would be a force to be reckoned with, whether I was furry or not. *Someone* had to boot the criminal element out of Shoreline.

Yuto wandered out into the parking lot to greet someone who'd pulled up in a minivan.

"Alone at last," Duncan said, amusement in his eyes.

"Just the way you want things with me?"

"Yup."

After parrying numerous attacks, I took the offensive and sent a few probing stabs in his direction. Duncan's technique was much different from Yuto's—he'd probably learned a European knightly way of fighting instead of being influenced by the Asian martial arts, but he didn't have any trouble deflecting my blows. Soon, we were alternating back and forth, and I appreciated the challenge, though I hadn't gotten as much rest as I might have liked and was soon panting, my hair damp, my shirt clinging to my torso.

Duncan wasn't breathing heavily, the bastard, though sweat did glisten on his chest. It nicely highlighted his muscles. The easy athleticism of his movements and the way they flexed and shifted was a touch mesmerizing. I would never admit it aloud, but his shirtless state *could* be distracting to female opponents. Too bad we couldn't...

Or could we?

The scar on Duncan's forehead hadn't glowed since the night I'd destroyed the control device that had been linked to it. If there was no danger of an enemy using magic to manipulate him—to force him to turn on me—couldn't I trust him enough to invite him into my bedroom? To be with him physically? To run my fingers along his strong jaw, brushing the three days' worth of beard growth that accented it, to touch my lips to his...

Unaware of the direction my thoughts had turned, Duncan pressed me. He picked up speed and launched a series of blows toward my head and chest. Though I managed to parry them, I caught myself backpedaling until my shoulder blades thumped against the wall. Caught without room to maneuver, I stabbed toward his chest, hoping to force him back.

He not only deflected my practice sword but caught my wrist and pressed it against the wall. I attempted to twist it to free myself, but his strength was greater than mine. And I... might not have wanted to escape. Especially when he leaned in close, his chest pressing against mine.

"Your allure has captured me, my lady." His gaze snagged on my lips.

"I believe I'm the one who's been captured." I looked pointedly at my trapped wrist.

"Do you mind?"

"Not as much as I should."

"Good." Duncan shifted closer, his lips finding mine.

They were hungry and demanding, as if he'd wanted this for a long time. That made me feel sexy and desirable—and not *old*, damn it. I was in the prime of my life. And Duncan wanted me.

His fingers loosened around my wrist, and I dropped the sword, eager to wrap my arms around his shoulders. I kissed him back, my lips just as hard and hungry as I tasted his masculine appeal, the salt of our sweat, the mingled heat of our desire. By the moon, I *did* want to invite him to my bedroom. Why had we waited so long? Why—

A phone rang. Mine. I didn't want to answer it, but a car door also slammed in the parking lot, a reminder that seven-year-olds in karate uniforms would soon wander into the dojo.

Reluctantly, I released Duncan's shoulders and patted him on the chest. He sighed, leaning back with equal reluctance. The passion burning in his brown eyes promised that he didn't want to release me. But he let me squirm out of his embrace, and I headed to the bench that held my belongings.

"Are you expecting an important call?" he asked.

"I'm expecting tart comments from my instructor if his grade-school students find us making out in the dojo."

"With your hand on my ass?"

"My hand wasn't there."

"It would have been." He grinned.

"So cocky and sure of yourself." I picked up the phone to see who had called.

Bolin. He was still at the apartment complex. I dialed him back.

"Is that a feature or a flaw?" Duncan grabbed his shirt but sat without putting it on, either to wait for his skin to dry or because he believed I preferred the display.

"Probably both. Hi, Bolin," I said as soon as he picked up. "What's up?"

"Uh, are you okay?"

Maybe a bit breathless, but... "Yeah. I've been working out."

Technically true. Duncan grinned again.

"Okay. Well, I thought you'd want to know right away..."

My bedroom thoughts evaporated as my stomach sank with the certainty of what he would say before he said it.

"There are a couple of serious buyers here at the complex. They're getting a tour, but they already said they're going to put in an offer. If it's as good as they're implying, I think my parents will accept it."

I sank down onto the bench as my earlier dark thoughts returned. I was about to lose my job and my home.

2

SINCE MY TRUCK WAS IN THE SHOP FOR REPAIRS—REPAIRS THAT HAD been required after enemies rammed it, hoping to send it hurtling down a mountainside—Duncan gave me a ride back to Sylvan Serenity.

As we drove in, I braced myself for an unfamiliar Lexus or BMW on the premises, the type of car driven by those with the means to make an offer on an apartment complex with more than two hundred units spread across several acres in a prime Seattle suburb.

But the hulking SUV parked next to Bolin's Mercedes G-Wagon was familiar, and, if Jasmine's research had been correct, cost a lot more than a run-of-the-mill luxury car. And why wouldn't it? With its military-upgrade package, it was not only armored but had night vision, EMP protection, and electrified door handles. I hadn't seen those in action, but I'd felt the impact —the *literal* impact—of its heavy-duty ram bumper.

"What the hell is that *thing* doing here?" I demanded from the passenger seat of Duncan's van, my knees up to my chin since his equipment occupied the foot space. Even though he'd only worked for Radomir and Abrams against his wishes, compelled by their magical control device, I couldn't keep from casting him an accusing look.

Duncan shook his head with puzzlement. "I don't know."

"If they came to rob me, they're too late. Some *other* thugs already handled that."

"You do still have the wolf case." Duncan parked in a different lane and turned off the engine. "They were never interested in the sword. They've only been collecting artifacts related to werewolves."

"I know all about their collection."

"They may have sent some of their potion-enhanced brutes to try to get the case from you," Duncan said, looking toward the SUV, "but I'm surprised they would do so during the day. They haven't yet been that open with their attacks."

I grumbled and jumped out, the urge to kick some asses creeping into me. More than that, the urge to turn *wolf* crept into me. Heat flushed my skin, and magic pricked all along my nerves.

Hand on the door, I took a deep breath to steady myself and willed the change to back off. This wasn't the time or place. A thought that became more true when I spotted Bolin and his parents—the owners of Sylvan Serenity and my employers—walking out of the leasing office. The last thing I needed was for them to see me change into a wolf in their parking lot.

But when two older men walked out behind them, the magic flared within me again. Radomir, his wispy hair appearing even thinner and paler in daylight, and the seventy-something Abrams, wearing a rumpled business suit that looked like it had been stored in a Mason jar. Maybe his medical scrubs and rubber gloves hadn't been deemed appropriate for this setting.

I shook my head. I hadn't seen them together since Duncan and I had broken into their lair at the lavender farm and potion factory in Arlington. Their brazenness in coming here openly galled me. Didn't they know they were *villains*? Villains were supposed to skulk about in the night, not stroll through an apartment complex in the middle of the day.

Fingers flexing, I stalked toward the sidewalk that bordered the parking lot. What I would say to them, I didn't know, but if I could get them away from the Sylvans and other witnesses, punching would be involved. Maybe clawing and biting—whether I changed or not.

Bolin noticed me and lifted a tentative hand, mouthing something as he tilted his head backward, toward the two older men. I squinted, not sure what that word had been. He mouthed it again.

"*Buyers.*"

I halted and gawked.

Radomir also noticed me, and he smiled, a smug knowing smile.

A door thumped, Duncan getting out of his van. He looked back and forth from Abrams and Radomir to me, his gaze lingering on me. He could probably sense how close I was to changing. He pointed his chin toward something in the street. A parked police car with two patrol officers in it. I'd almost forgotten it was there. The police had been keeping an eye on the place because of the increased crime of late.

That meant I couldn't get away with punching, biting, or anything else deemed illegal, not today.

"Ah, there's our star property manager." Rory Sylvan lifted a hand toward me. "She keeps costs low by handling numerous duties herself and has been integral in this complex's success over the years."

Normally, the accolade would have delighted me, but it was all I could do to keep from snarling as I walked stiffly toward the group.

Kashvi Sylvan, always the supreme professional businesswoman, didn't smile and wasn't as warm, but she did nod in my direction and say, "Ms. Valens had been a boon and doubtless knows the buildings backward and forward. Should you wish to keep her on, I believe she desires to stay."

Radomir and Abrams regarded me, Abrams squinting as if I were a strange bug to examine under a magnifying glass. Radomir... still looked smug.

"Thank you," I managed to murmur to the Sylvans.

"We'll do a background check on her and consider it," Radomir said grandly.

I barely kept from gagging. As if I would work for them, even if their offer was legitimate.

No. I rocked back. There was no *way* their offer was legitimate. They ran a huge *potion* business. None of the addresses that Jasmine's dad had looked up were multifamily investments. They had farms and warehouses and weird little mushroom grow labs in rustic cabins in the foothills of the Cascades.

"These are the buyers?" I asked Bolin and looked around, half-expecting to have reached the wrong assumption. Maybe they'd come *posing* as buyers, because it was open-house day or some such, and someone else had put in the offer that Bolin had mentioned.

Bolin shrugged. "Yes."

"We like what we see and plan to make an offer." Radomir nodded to the Sylvans.

My roving gaze—my *confused* gaze—landed on Duncan. He had stopped near the SUVs and stood with his arms folded over his chest as he watched the group and listened. His gaze lingered on Abrams, the man who'd raised him in a time long ago and a place far away. The man who'd *made* him, taking genetic material from a centuries-dead werewolf who'd been buried under a glacier. Duncan knew Abrams far better than I did, but I didn't need to consult with him to know the scientist had zero interest in becoming a landlord.

"We'll certainly consider it," Kashvi said. "Is there anything else you'd like to see before you go?"

"Perhaps a couple of the units if you have any vacancies?" Radomir pointed in the direction of *my* building.

Because he hoped for a tour of my apartment? And a chance to snoop and see if the wolf case was in there?

Unfortunately, it was. Radomir was, as far as I'd been able to tell, a mundane human being, but he wore rings that emanated power, and I suspected one might let him sense magic—and magical artifacts—if he drew near them.

"I emptied out D-21 and will be getting it ready for a new tenant soon." I pointed toward the farthest building back, one nowhere near mine.

My alchemist associate, Rue, lived a few units from the vacant apartment, and I silently apologized to her for sending these jerks in her direction. But maybe she would sense their evilness and toss some poisonous potions at them. Oh, and hadn't she mentioned a concoction that could cause genital warts? Would it be wrong of me to text and ask her to prepare a couple of doses of that?

"This way." Rory waved for the two men to follow him. "Those units are nice. They have a view of the grounds and trees. I did the original renovations on them back in the eighties."

Though I was positive Radomir and Abrams had no interest in views of the grounds, they followed Rory without objection. Kashvi received a phone call and walked off to answer it privately. I took the opportunity to pounce on Bolin.

"Those aren't *really* the buyers, are they?" I whispered since his mother remained in the area.

"Yes, they're the ones who plan to put in an offer. You recognized them?"

"Faster than you would a word with Greek roots at a spelling bee."

"I'd object to that, since that's not even a challenge, but you did seem instantly perturbed when you saw them."

"*Instantly.*"

Bolin was lucky I hadn't changed into a wolf in the parking lot. We all were. Though... it might have been worth it to get the Radomir-and-Abrams problem out of my life. But, no. If I ended up in jail for murder, that would be a whole new problem.

"They're evil overlords," I added. "You might even have seen Radomir up at that vacation cabin. He was in the tank SUV. *That* tank SUV." I thrust my arm toward it.

"I came out of the cabin after the fight out front was over. There weren't any cars there then. Or tanks. Just a wolf and... a hulking *two*-legged werewolf." Bolin looked at me, as if *I* were the problem here today.

"Yes, a bipedfuris." I glanced toward Duncan. "That's not important. That we had to fight Radomir and his thugs because he kidnapped my son is. They're *bad guys*. They don't want to buy an apartment complex. Trust me."

"You don't think the nefariously inclined invest in multifamily properties?"

"*No.*"

Bolin pointed to the armored tank-SUV. "How else would they afford a Rezvani?"

"Leave it to you to be able to recognize a ridiculously priced car."

"The name is on the front grill."

"I'll bet you knew what it was before it rolled in."

"Maybe. I *am* a guy." Bolin flattened his hand on his chest as if that explained why he knew about expensive vehicles.

"You play classical music on your violin, compete in spelling bees, and have 3D-printed dragons."

He narrowed his eyes. "Hobbies that don't negate my *maleness*."

I sighed. "Okay, sorry. You're right. That was low, but I'm frustrated. Not only are they not legitimate buyers, but they're dangerous."

"I also, as you'll recall, can play rap beats on my violin. Masculinely."

"Yes, yes, your beats were very assertive and testosterone-fueled. Listen, those guys are probably only here because they want an excuse to openly scope out the place and find the wolf case." Remembering that he'd had an unpleasant encounter with one of their minions, I added, "They're the ones who hired that thug who hurled you into a post."

"Oh, I don't like them then."

"*Good.*"

"I had to go to the ER." Bolin touched his eyebrow, the scar remaining though the stitches had long since been removed. For the first time, his expression turned troubled as he gazed in the direction his father had led Radomir and Abrams.

I glanced at the parking lot again, but Duncan had disappeared. Maybe he was spying on them. I *hoped* he was spying on them.

Kashvi came over, holding her phone out toward Bolin. "I talked to our agent. Their offer came in and is exactly what we're asking."

"Better make sure they included proof of funds," I said.

"Of course, and they did." Kashvi nodded. "I'll tell Rory."

As she headed toward the back of the complex, Bolin spread his arms. "Maybe they're legitimate buyers."

"They're not," I said. "I promise. They're criminals."

"If so, they're very well-off criminals. The asking price for this complex is substantial."

"If only I could imagine how criminals would acquire piles of money. And priceless werewolf artifacts."

Bolin sighed. "My parents were talking about being able to retire and relax more if this goes through. In a year or two, after

I've got more experience, they could see letting me run the daily operations of the whole business. I could finally travel to their various complexes around the world and have a real career. And —" his eyes grew sharp with imagined pleasure, "—if my brother wants to be involved, I would be in charge of him."

"You've got a vendetta against your brother?" I remembered Bolin talking about how they'd wrestled as kids and knocked over a candle. The story hadn't led me to imagine them being terribly rambunctious or antagonistic. "Isn't he younger than you?"

"Yeah, but he's athletic and confident about everything and has..." Bolin groped in the air. "*Je ne sais quoi.*" He made a face. "Girls in school send him notes *all* the time."

"Probably because he doesn't say geeky things like *je ne sais quoi.*"

"Oh, he does. He's got the family smarts too. It's exceedingly obnoxious."

"So, you naturally want to be his boss."

"*Yes.*"

"If your smirk gets any more gleeful, I'm going to classify you with the two evil overlords."

"I wouldn't be mean to him. Just... superior."

I sighed, far more concerned about Radomir and Abrams than the family dynamics of my intern. "Look, Bolin. That isn't a legit offer. Your parents aren't going to get to retire this month. If you're as smart as you think you are, you'll nose around and look those two up. You'll see that they don't have any other multifamily properties. They don't want to be landlords."

I opened my mouth to argue further, but Bolin held a finger to his lips and nodded past my shoulder. Rory was returning with Kashvi, Radomir, and Abrams. I clamped my mouth shut, though I didn't care that much if those two learned I wanted to thwart their scheme. They had to know I would warn everyone who would listen.

As they approached, movement on the rooftop of the building they'd left caught my eye. Duncan crouched up there, peering over the crest.

Hah. He *had* been spying on them.

I hoped he'd learned something useful, though he probably hadn't. Since Rory had presumably been with Radomir and Abrams the whole time, they wouldn't have said anything to give away their ruse.

Kashvi led the group into the leasing office, but Abrams deviated, heading toward me. I tensed and glanced toward Duncan, but he ducked out of view. Abrams also looked toward the rooftop but not in time to spot him.

"Ms. Valens, was it?" he asked, stopping in front of me.

"You know damn well who I am. You and your buddy have been stalking me—and my family's artifacts—for weeks." Technically, the wolf case wasn't a family artifact and didn't, as far as I knew, have anything to do with my pack, but it at least had to do with werewolves. Yes, it *protected* the holder from werewolves instead of working on behalf of our kind, but it was in the ballpark. And these two wanted it.

"I'm certain I don't know what you're talking about," Abrams said blandly with a much less charming version of Duncan's accent.

"Bolin knows who you are. He was *at* the cabin when Radomir charged in and tried to get Duncan to attack me and my son."

Bolin opened his mouth, probably to remind me that he hadn't seen Radomir. I glared at him, and he closed it again.

"That sounds like a fanciful accounting from a fictional tale," Abrams said.

"Uh-huh. What the hell do you two want? And what's up with the big charade? *Most* people who want my stuff just rob my apartment to get it."

"Is that an invitation?" Abrams asked.

"*No*. You wouldn't find any artifacts in there anyway."

That was sort of true. I'd given Mom's magical medallion back to her, and the wolf case was in the heat duct *under* the apartment, not inside of it.

"I see." Abrams looked at Bolin, then inclined his head in the opposite direction. "Might I chat with you briefly in private, Ms. Valens?"

"Do you want to interview me for a possible property-management position should you buy this complex?"

"We *would* like to know more about your qualifications."

"Right."

Even though I wanted to punch Abrams, not *chat* with him, it would be silly to pass up the opportunity to learn something. Reluctantly, I trailed him to a private spot under a tree, the birds chirping cheerfully in the branches, unaware that the fate of their home lay in the balance.

"Radomir told me what you did." Apparently, Abrams wasn't one for small talk.

That suited me fine. "It's so nice that you two are buddies and can confide in each other."

"You were the one to destroy the *dux*."

"Is that the device that could manipulate Duncan? Call him from far away and force him to do *evil* shit?"

Last time, it had only forced him to hunt for a magical medallion, but Duncan had spoken of the past, of the unpleasantries Abrams had once made him do.

"It was inextricably linked to him at birth," Abrams said.

"Well, it's unlinked now."

His lips pressed together in a thin line. "Yes. And with that, you've marked his fate."

I'd been on the verge of feeling smug that I'd destroyed his ability to control Duncan, but, as the words sank in, I started to worry. What was Abrams implying?

Originally, I'd intended to *steal* the control device, not bite it to pieces. Even knowing nothing about how the magic worked, I'd worried that destroying it would have ramifications, that it might hurt Duncan. Of course, in my furry state, with the savagery of the wolf flowing into me, I hadn't been able to think about such complex concepts.

"What fate?" I asked warily when Abrams didn't continue on his own.

"The magic of the *dux* tapped into Drakon's life force. The abrupt breaking of the link..." Abrams shook his head and looked toward the rooftop where Duncan had crouched. Abrams's brow creased, and he almost looked as though Duncan's fate still mattered to him, like he *cared*.

If I hadn't been worried, I would have scoffed. This guy had ordered Duncan tossed naked into a ditch. Abrams *wanted* him dead. At least according to Duncan. Only Radomir, because he'd wanted to use Duncan for his artifact-gathering plans, had decided on a less fatal disposal.

"His life force will wither—all of him will—as if he were a plant whose roots have all been severed. Within a week, maybe two, he will die."

"He's not dying. I just talked to him—and sparred with him. He's *fine*."

"It will start slowly, deep within him." Abrams touched his forehead, near where Duncan's scar was. "Then it will accelerate as his end approaches." He looked back at me, frowning. "As I said, you've sealed his fate."

I froze my face, not wanting to react, to show him that he'd worried me, but I longed to reel back, to deny that I'd been responsible for breaking the device. I had been, however. The *wolf* in me had been. But the wolf hadn't known. *I* hadn't known.

I wanted to tell Abrams to beat it and to knock off whatever scheme he and Radomir were enacting, but he was the only one who had answers, answers I now craved. "How do we reverse things and make sure Duncan doesn't die?"

"There is no way. The *dux* was an ancient tool from another time, from when magic was more abundant in the earth and powerful craftsmen could make such devices. As far as I know, there isn't another like that one remaining in existence."

Radomir walked out of the leasing office and nodded to Abrams.

"Your recklessness ensures that Drakon dies within weeks," Abrams said before turning away from me.

Guilt slammed into me, but my response was to snarl. "You're the one who was controlling him, who *linked* him to that thing, you bastard. Don't blame this on me."

My fingers curled into fists and I almost sprang upon Abrams, longing to strangle him and demand more satisfying answers. He knew more than he was telling me. There had to be a way to help Duncan.

But Rory and Kashvi walked out of the leasing office, and I remembered the police car parked out front. I couldn't strangle people that the world believed were upright businessmen in the middle of a legitimate transaction.

"If he dies, it'll be *your* fault," I growled as Abrams walked away.

He didn't look back. He didn't believe that. Unfortunately, my heart wouldn't let me believe it either. If Duncan died, it would be because of me.

3

As Abrams and Radomir drove away in their tank-SUV, and the Sylvans stepped into their own car, I bent forward on the walkway, gripping my knees. I wanted to throw up.

"He may have been lying," came Duncan's voice as he walked up, appearing from behind whatever bush or lamppost had hidden him while he listened.

I couldn't blame him for eavesdropping. It had been his fate Abrams had been talking about.

"Did your spying reveal something that would suggest that?" I asked hopefully, straightening and facing him.

"No. They were in your employer's presence most of the time that I was listening." Duncan pointed to the rooftop where he'd perched. "Only once did they speak of anything besides their fictitious plans to acquire this compound. Abrams asked Radomir if he could detect *it* here. I assume he referred to the wolf case—specifically, the artifact within it. They likely know I have the male version of the Medallion of Memory and Power and that you returned the female version to your mother, so they wouldn't be seeking those here."

"Yeah." Not worried about the artifacts at the moment, I studied Duncan's face, trying to decide if he appeared concerned about his *life force* withering. Did he believe what Abrams had said?

I couldn't tell. He didn't seem to be masking his features. His expression was calm, as if we were discussing the weather. Or, I supposed, artifacts.

"How's your life force?" I asked.

My voice almost cracked on the term. That worry and guilt hadn't left. If anything, having Duncan in front of me made the feelings stronger, and my throat grew tight.

He turned his palm toward the sky. "I feel hale."

"You *seemed* hale in the dojo when you were flattening me to the wall."

"You say that as if you didn't enjoy the flattening."

My cheeks heated. I had enjoyed it. And he knew it.

"It was a good way to assess your health," I said. "Your life force."

"Is that what you were doing when you slid your tongue into my mouth?"

"Yeah, it's called probing. Medical professionals do it all the time."

"Usually with less evocative instruments."

"*Duncan*," I said, my emotions bubbling over. "I'm sorry I destroyed that thing. All I ever wanted to do was steal it so they couldn't use it to control you anymore."

"That was your plan from the beginning? When you wanted to follow me up there?"

I hadn't mentioned that goal to him, worried he would stop me because he believed it too dangerous. Now, I wished I *had* asked him about the control device. He might have known he was linked to it, that destroying it could kill him. At least according to Abrams. Thus far, Duncan seemed skeptical about that.

"It was," I said. "I should have told you."

"I thought it might be something like that. You wanted to help me. I can't be upset about that."

"Yes, you can. I didn't intend this. It was a mistake. Like I said, I only wanted to take that device—there's nothing wrong with thieving from thieves, right?"

"It does seem fair." Duncan smiled and stepped forward to hug me.

It was a gentle embrace, almost as if he needed support as much as I did. This time, there was no probing on either of our parts. I leaned my face against his shoulder, and he stroked the back of my head.

For a while, we stood like that, the birds chirping cheerfully, the freeway traffic audible but muted through the trees. In the street, the police car left as another arrived to take its spot.

"Change of shift," I murmured.

A parcel-delivery van rolled into the lot. Assuming it was bringing something for a tenant, I didn't think anything of it until the driver stepped out with a cardboard overnight-delivery envelope and headed toward the Roadtrek.

Duncan sighed as the guy tucked it under a windshield wiper and marked the task as complete on his electronic device. It wasn't the first time something had been delivered to Duncan's van. Last time, it had been poisoned chocolate.

"Do you want to see what that is?" I asked.

"No." Duncan also had to be thinking about the poisoned chocolate.

But my cousin who'd masterminded that plot was dead. This had to be something else.

Despite his *no*, Duncan released me and headed to the van. I went with him, afraid this had to do with Radomir and Abrams.

As the delivery vehicle drove away, Duncan opened the envelope and withdrew a single piece of paper with a letter typed on it. He let me read it over his arm.

Mr. Calderwood,

Your lady acquaintance has done us no favors by destroying the device that was linked to you. Lord Abrams has informed me that it is—that it was—bound to your life and that you'll soon die. Since you've proven useful, though you were recalcitrant at times and failed to bring the correct medallion to me, I do not wish that fate for you. We might yet work together for the betterment not only of the werewolf species but of mankind as a whole. As my own mortality makes itself known, my so-called golden years drawing nearer, I seek to leave a legacy, to help people.

"Bullshit." I hadn't finished reading the letter, but I'd glanced down at the signature. It was Radomir. "That guy's trying to make money, *more* money, or something else. He doesn't care about mankind. And his thugs shot up my mom's home—and my mom. No way does he care about werewolves."

Duncan grunted in agreement and tilted the page so that I could more easily read the rest.

I've asked Lord Abrams if, with all the knowledge he's accumulated over the years, he's aware of something that might prevent a deadly fate for you. You deserve better. I'm most perturbed with your lady acquaintance.

"Like I give a shit," I muttered but kept reading.

.   .   .

Abrams is not certain there is a solution but believes that, given enough powerful artifacts to work with, a crafter might be found who could make something capable of healing the broken link and saving your life. I'll use my connections to seek out such a person. In the meantime, I need you to bring to me the two wolf-head medallions and the wolf-lidded case with its special tool inside. These artifacts, we believe, may have the power we need, power that could be siphoned into a new artifact, one capable of saving your life. Do not take too long to bring them to me. I understand that once your life force is sufficiently withered, the effects are more difficult to reverse, that we will not be able to halt your demise

Sincerely,

~ Ivan Radomir

"What a liar. Both of them." I shook my head and leaned back. "Like those three specific artifacts that they've been trying to find or steal would happen to be the ones that could help you."

Duncan, jaw set as he continued to gaze down at the letter, didn't answer. His eyes weren't moving, so he'd stopped reading.

"There's no way that's anything but bullshit." I watched his face. "Right?"

He folded the letter and returned it to the envelope. "I agree that it's unlikely."

"If I thought they *would* do what he said..."

I swallowed. What? I would hand them over to Radomir? I could give up the wolf case—that wasn't mine, nor did I know who the true owner was. Someone long dead, probably. But the medallions? Those belonged to the pack, not me. I supposed if Duncan's life truly depended on it, I would ask for Mom's medallion—or take it—but I didn't trust Radomir.

"If you're really dying, I'd do anything to help you," I said, "but this has to be a set-up, don't you think? We can't trust these guys."

"No." Duncan managed a smile for me. "You'd do anything to save my life? I'm touched."

"Of course. You're..."

He raised his eyebrows. "Appealingly charismatic and desirable?"

"You *know* that. You're also... I like you." Not exactly a confession of love, but my emotions were all tangled up. After being betrayed by my ex, my natural inclination was to be private, not to voice words that could be turned against me.

"I like you as well." Once more, Duncan drew me into a hug, resting his cheek against my hair. "We should cruise around town and try to find the thugs who stole your sword. Now that you're a master, you should be wielding it instead of dented wood."

"I'm a master after six lessons?"

"You're doing well."

"I do want to find it, but that *can't* be the most important thing on your mind right now."

I recalled my vow to quaff that awful-tasting potion, the Elixir of Locus that Rue had made. I had only asked her for one attuned to Duncan, but she'd taken a blood sample from one of the thugs who'd attacked us in the parking lot and made a second one. We'd thought he might be from the same gang as those who'd robbed my apartment to steal the sword. If I could stomach chugging the loathsome potion, and I was within ten miles of him, it ought to lead me to him. It was the ten-mile radius as well as the horrible taste that had made me hesitate to take it right away.

"I would like to see it back in your hand," Duncan said, "before... before long."

That hesitation made me lean back and look into his eyes. "Before you *die*? You said you thought Abrams might be lying about all that and that your *life force* feels fine."

"Oh, yes. It's quite lovely. And I believe it is quite possible that they're lying to manipulate us." Duncan smiled easily, and I couldn't tell if he was prevaricating or not.

What if he simply didn't want me to worry? Might he believe that Abrams *had* been telling the truth?

"My life, however, has been somewhat dangerous of late," Duncan said. "In truth, I've always been known to take a risk or two in my pursuit of adventure and treasure."

"You did mention swimming with killer whales that wear salmon hats."

"I did, though that wasn't the riskiest thing I've done, not by far. The whale was quite amiable."

"As sea life showing off the latest fashions so often are."

"Indeed. Since, however, I do take those risks... Well, just in case, I'd like to see the sword back in your hands before my passing."

Glum, I continued to gaze at him. The barbells of certainty thumped down on my shoulders. He *did* believe he would die. And not in some vague years-off future but soon. Because of the device I'd destroyed.

Tears welled in my eyes. I looked away so he wouldn't see them. "Duncan..."

The door to the police car thumped shut, and he didn't respond. Officer Dubois had been in the replacement vehicle, and she jogged toward us, a partner I hadn't met before remaining in the passenger seat. She'd lost her *last* partner in the parking lot the night Duncan and I had turned into wolves to defend the property from thugs. Dubois had seen me shift, but she hadn't brought it up, other than to say she owed me. I wouldn't assume there were no stipulations on her secrecy, but seeing her didn't make me wince and want to run in the other direction anymore.

Her pace remaining brisk, she headed straight toward us. "We've had a report of a robbery and need to leave to offer backup over at Rocket Coffee."

"Uh-oh. That's my intern's favorite spot."

"Big guys on motorcycles is what I heard." Dubois looked grimly at me. "Your place won't be covered until we return. I wanted to warn you."

"Let me know if you see any familiar brutish faces over there." I lifted a hand since she was already turning to jog back to her car. I hadn't expected the police to provide 24-7 coverage of Sylvan Serenity anyway.

"You miss them?" Dubois called over her shoulder.

"Like a rash on my ass, yeah."

She waved an acknowledgment, then slid back into her car and took off.

"If it *is* the same guys," I told Duncan, who was watching me curiously, "including the one Rue's potion is linked to, I could take it, and we could follow them to their hideout."

I had no idea if they *had* a hideout. Maybe the thugs all had their own apartments. Even if that was the case, the one we'd gotten the blood sample from might know where his buddies had stashed the sword.

"We could go to the coffee shop, turn into wolves, and trail them to their hideout the old-fashioned way." Duncan tapped his nose.

"As I recall, you tried that before and were stymied when they got into a getaway car and drove away."

"I wasn't stymied. I lost the scent."

"Thus stymying you." I didn't blame him. I would have had even more trouble following their trail through the city.

"It's impossible to track an automobile far."

"Unless a potion that burns your esophagus like a hell-born inferno magically guides you in the right direction."

"I've not had that experience, but I'll take your word for it."

"You can drink the next potion if you want to endure it yourself."

"To retrieve the sword, I would."

I waved away his offer. As awful as the potion was, I wouldn't wish the side effects on anyone else. "I'll do it."

And I would. I owed it to him to find the sword he'd given me. But I was a lot more worried about Duncan's life force and what Radomir and Abrams were up to with their offer on Sylvan Serenity.

4

PERCHED ON A LADDER, I WAS FIXING A TENANT'S BROKEN WINDOW seal, worrying about Duncan and waiting to see if Dubois would call, when Bolin returned. He wasn't with his parents—or their prospective buyers—this time, but he held a newspaper under one arm, so I wasn't relieved. The last time he'd shared a story with me, it hadn't been anything good. It had highlighted the deaths—*murders*, as the reporter had called them—in our parking lot and speculated that a wolf had been involved.

"What?" I asked warily, climbing down from the ladder.

"I spotted a story that might interest you."

"For a Gen Z'er, you spend a lot of time scouring physical newspapers." I accepted the offering, a short article halfway down the page circled.

"I have online alerts set up for a few keyword searches. When this popped up, I went out to find a physical paper to bring to you. I know Boomers struggle with opening links and reading things on their phones." His tone was teasing, a smirk finding his lips.

"You *know* I'm not a Boomer. I'm barely Gen X."

His gaze drifted to my hairline. Damn it, I *did* need to make time for a dye session.

"I hope you have keyword searches set up for Radomir, Abrams, and their corporation that has absolutely nothing to do with multifamily properties, so they don't bamboozle your parents." I scowled at Bolin before lifting the paper, not holding it as close to my eyes as I would if I didn't have a young and irreverent witness—how come my vision was perfect as a wolf, but letters were fuzzy when I was in my human form?

"I'm looking into them further." Bolin sounded serious.

"Good." I skimmed an article about a robbery in Bellevue, expecting it to tie in to the motorcycle thugs and *my* robbery. But all it mentioned was that the penthouse condominium of a well-to-do real estate mogul had been broken into and a precious antique stolen from a vault. "Oh," I said when I reached the end.

According to the victim, the antique had been a golden bracelet that featured a wolf head on the top. It had been an heirloom purchased from a collector in Europe decades earlier.

"It looks like Radomir and Abrams are still pilfering priceless artifacts related to werewolves," I said.

"I wondered if it might be the same people who've been sending thugs after you." Bolin touched his scar. "And anyone in your orbit."

"Anyone in my orbit carrying a wolf-lidded case, yeah. And *of course* it's those two. I'm sure it hasn't suddenly gotten trendy for criminals throughout the Puget Sound area to steal magical werewolf jewelry."

"The article doesn't mention if this was magical but..."

"Reporters are notorious for leaving out those details," I said.

Outside of the paranormal community, few acknowledged that magic existed. Since normal humans couldn't usually sense it, that wasn't surprising.

"Thanks for sharing." I couldn't imagine how I could use the information, so I handed the newspaper back to Bolin. Maybe it might prove fruitful to talk to the victim and ask for details about the artifact—and if a security camera had caught footage of the thieves—but I doubted it would do more than confirm that Radomir and Abrams were still collecting.

"You're welcome. I also took a picture of this when our prospective buyers were parked here." Bolin tapped his phone to pull up a photo.

"You think my ancient geriatric eyes will be able to see it?" I asked dryly.

"I can use the zoom," he said, deadpan, then held up the phone to show a license plate.

I wouldn't have guessed the significance except that the fender looked familiar. Ah, yes. It had rammed my truck.

"Since you're friends with the police now," Bolin said, "I thought they might look up the address of the owner of the car for you."

"Dubois and I aren't *that* close. And I doubt it's Radomir's home address anyway. It sounds like he's been hopping hideouts lately. The bastard *knows* I'd like to hunt him down." Despite my words, I held up a finger and pulled out my own phone for a call.

Bolin raised his eyebrows.

My niece, Jasmine, answered.

"Hey, girl. Any progress with the job hunt?" I felt I should ask about her life before requesting more favors. She'd helped me a lot of late, and all I'd been able to do in return was agree to be a reference for her résumé.

"I've had a couple of interviews but no offers yet. Apparently, the real estate business is slow everywhere. Nobody's buying since prices are high, and interest rates are up."

"That's probably why lots of people are applying for apartments at Sylvan Serenity instead of buying condos. Despite all the reports of odd things happening here, this is a lot more affordable than a mortgage right now."

"Odd as in murders and werewolves? Or as in a druidic guy who blows up an inflatable garage to protect his hoity-toity SUV from bird poop?"

I didn't think her tone conveyed that she was falling in love with the druidic guy, despite his attempt to serenade her with rap beats. Poor Bolin.

Aware of him watching—hopefully he couldn't *hear* the conversation—I held up a finger and took a few steps away.

"Bolin is more quirky than odd," I told Jasmine, "and only the werewolves and murders have made it into the papers."

"Well, they're not as much of a deterrent as you'd think." Jasmine didn't comment on adjectives appropriate for Bolin. "An affordable price is an affordable price. You guys are actually a little below-market on rents. Did you know? Besides, it's not like the werewolves bother anyone except hoodlums, vandals, and the occasional plump and delectable rabbit."

"Something the newspapers always fail to mention." I cleared my throat. "I called to ask for another favor."

"What do you want my dad to look up now?"

"Can he use his elite computer skills to find an address associated with a license-plate number?"

"I don't think that's legal, but that's not what you asked."

I hesitated. "I don't want to get him in trouble."

"He and Mom donate to the National Fraternal Order of Police, and he also helped solve three crimes in the last ten years by analyzing imagery from public traffic cameras to get faces and license plates of miscreants that nobody else caught."

"Does that mean that even if he got caught snooping in the DMV's database, he might not get in trouble?"

"I wouldn't think so, but I couldn't say for sure. Text me the license plate number, and I'll ask him."

"Is that Jasmine?" Bolin whispered, not stepping closer but *leaning* closer, as if drawn by her magnetism oozing through the phone.

"Yeah, she wants you to send that license-plate photo."

"Who's there?" Jasmine asked.

"Bolin."

"Oh, did he hear me making fun of his blow-up garage?"

"I'm not sure, but, if it helps, I make fun of it frequently. Also the plastic owls he used as his *first* attempt at a bird-poop deterrent." I smiled at Bolin.

He frowned at me.

"Tell him I was just teasing," Jasmine said. "I've seen weirder things. He's an okay guy. Good taste in music."

I didn't mention that Bolin would ensure his taste matched exactly whatever her taste was. "Yeah, he's decent."

Bolin's frown faded, his eyebrows rising hopefully. I made button-pushing motions in the air.

"I don't have her number," he whispered.

"Jasmine, is it okay if I give Bolin your number? He's the one with the photo of the license plate." Sure, I could have asked Bolin to send it to me, then relayed it to her, but... I owed Bolin a few. I doubted he would pester Jasmine relentlessly with memes about love and adoration, and maybe this would open up the line of communications.

"Oh, sure." She didn't sound worried about him having her number. That was promising.

As he sent the photo to her, a text came in on my phone, another photo. It was from Dubois and showed a police officer arresting a bearded man in black leather and another officer chasing a guy with a similar look who'd been in the process of springing over a car in the coffee-shop drive-thru to get away. They were both familiar. The one escaping...

"That's the one I have a potion for," I blurted.

Bolin looked up from his phone. "IIm?"

"Nothing. I need to find Duncan." And grab Rue's potion from my apartment.

"On my way here, I saw him dangling a rope into a koi pond in the courtyard of the condos on the corner."

To think, Jasmine thought *Bolin* was the odd one around here.

"The rope has a magnet on the end," I explained.

"Thus making his actions... normal?"

"I didn't say that."

5

Aware that it wouldn't take the thug long to escape my potion's ten-mile radius, especially if he got on a motorcycle, I grabbed the vial and raced down the street to collect Duncan. As Bolin had said, Duncan perched by a koi pond, plucking a set of keys off his magnet while the fish hid on the far side from him.

"The local thugs robbed Rocket Coffee." I waved for him to join me.

"The same thugs who took your sword?" Duncan laid the keys on the stone wall framing the pond and trotted over to join me. He wound his rope around the damp magnet and stuffed it all into a jacket pocket.

"I don't know if they were involved in my robbery, but I'll bet this one knows who was." I held up my phone with the photo that Dubois had sent.

"And will be happy to tell us?"

"If my hand is around his throat, absolutely."

"I do love a woman with a brutish streak." Duncan grinned at me.

Since the coffee shop wasn't far, we hoofed it. By the time we arrived, the police cars had left, and there was no sign of the thugs. I hoped at least one was on his way to jail.

When I texted Dubois, she admitted that the one who'd been leaping the drive-thru cars had escaped, but she had people out looking for him. Two other thugs *had* been captured and were on their way to the station for questioning.

"Our guy is still on the loose." I held up the Elixir of Locus with a determined grimace. "Let's hope this works." I bared my teeth at the vial, working up the stomach fortitude to chug it.

"It must be as bad as you said if not worse," Duncan commented, watching my face.

"Oh, it is."

As I thumbed off the cork, Duncan walked up to the drive-thru window to examine the menu. The burglary hadn't prompted the barista—or maybe that was the owner—to close the business. Even as I watched, three cars turned off the street and veered for the drive-thru, getting in line behind Duncan. In the Seattle area, it took a lot to stop the delivery of espresso to caffeine-addicted consumers.

Tears threatening before I lifted the vial to my lips, I tilted my head back, pinched my nostrils shut, and dumped the contents down my throat.

The viscous slug-slime-like liquid was as bad as I remembered. Maybe worse. It burned my throat like a propane-fueled weed-killing torch, and I struggled not to cough the potion back up as tears streamed down my cheeks and my esophagus undulated in distress.

Hell, was a magical sword worth this? If it hadn't been a gift from Duncan, and I hadn't felt so bad about losing it, I would have uttered a vehement *no*. Not that I could utter anything at the moment.

Duncan returned to my side. "That's a dreadful sacrifice you're making, my lady."

"Tell... me... about it..." I rasped.

Wiping my eyes, I stood and took a couple of deep, shuddering breaths. If it was like last time, I would have heartburn for a few minutes before my esophagus started tingling and guiding me in the direction of our target.

Duncan stood with two different types of bottled water in his hands, as well as a caramel mocha.

"To help you wash that down," he offered.

I took a swig from a carbonated water, then sipped the mocha and swished it around in my mouth. Normally, I didn't drink anything that sweet, but, at that moment, I would have chugged a Yoo-hoo with a Snickers bar floating in it. Anything to get rid of the taste.

As I drank and wiped my eyes again, Duncan delved into a pocket. He pulled out a bag of white- and brown-speckled chocolate-covered coffee beans.

"Did you order one of everything on the menu?" I accepted the candies as he poured them into my hand.

"Almost. You looked like you needed a lot to wash that down. And possibly a visit to the ER."

"I'll pass on that." I crunched down the sweet beans. "A doctor might notice the strangeness of my blood." I grimaced at the growing pain in my chest. The candy beans and mocha helped flush the foul taste out of my mouth, but they couldn't assist with the heartburn. "After all this, our brute had better not be more than ten miles away."

After another swig of the mocha, I thanked Duncan for getting all the items for me. My esophagus started tingling. It was the same sensation as the last time I'd drunk one of the potions and accompanied by an urge to turn my chest in the direction of the freeway.

"It's going to work," I whispered, pointing.

"Excellent. Can you tell how far away he is? Do you want me to get my van?"

"I can't tell that, no, but... my tingling chest insists that I go that way." Worried the guy would move out of range if we delayed, I hurried off on foot, clutching the mocha and water bottle.

Duncan looked toward Sylvan Serenity for a moment, then decided to trot after me. I didn't know if eschewing the van was the right decision or not, but the tingling led me to cut down an alley, through an unfenced backyard, and around thorny blackberry brambles.

Had the thug gone this way? Maybe the potion was simply pointing me along the most direct route to catch up to him.

Duncan matched my pace, turning when I turned and cursing at the thorns when I cursed—actually, he called them *cheeky little buggers*.

"What happens if we have to cross the freeway?" he asked when the rumble of traffic grew louder.

"We'll get to test our abilities to dodge six lanes of traffic whizzing by at sixty miles per hour."

Duncan slanted me a look. "From what I've observed of the gridlock freeway traffic here, we're more likely to encounter an unmoving car park."

"That'll make dodging easier."

Before we reached the freeway, the tingling prompted me to turn parallel to it, jogging through trees and parking lots. To one side, a light-rail train whizzed past. Before the station came into view, I had an inkling of where we were going.

"Huh."

"Huh?" Duncan asked.

"The potion might be leading me along the exact route he took rather than pointing me in the vague direction of his current location." I gestured to the back of the station, the tracks heading to it.

"Then I'll hope he was as scraped up by those thorny brambles as we were."

"Maybe he was *more* scraped up. He's a big guy."

The tingling wanted me to go through a back door of the train station, but I opted for the front. Inside, commuters were standing ready to get on the next train. I hoped to spot the thug in one of the queues—or, more likely, brutalizing people as he shoved them aside to cut to the front—but didn't see him. I got the sense from the tingling, which wanted to draw me south as well as toward the doors leading to the tracks, that he'd already departed.

My feet led me to one of the doors as a train pulled in, but I halted.

"I didn't bring my purse." Not that it would have mattered. I hadn't taken public transportation in a while and doubted my ORCA card had any money on it.

"Allow me, my lady." Duncan stepped forward, fingers delving into his pockets.

My first thought was that he meant to use his magnet to trick the pay machines into letting us pass, but he fished out handfuls of change. *Damp* change.

"Is that from the koi pond?"

Duncan grinned at me as he fed coins into the machine. People behind us in line sighed at the slowness of using physical currency, especially currency dropped in one dime or quarter at a time.

"I thought you said American money isn't magnetic," I said.

"It's not, but the pond wasn't deep."

"You fished out coins people threw in to make their wishes come true? That's kind of..."

"Noble." Duncan waved us through when the machine indicated we'd paid enough for two fares.

"Noble?"

"Coins can be toxic to fish, even those not large enough to accidentally eat them. They corrode and release metals into the water."

I squinted at him, wondering if he'd made that up.

"I read a news story once," Duncan continued as we boarded, "that a turtle in Bangkok died from blood poisoning in such a pond."

"Are you sure you just didn't want a coffee and you forgot your wallet in your van?"

He grinned again. "I believe the mocha and chocolates *did* come in handy when you needed to wash that dreadful potion from your mouth."

"Does that make me an accomplice to your theft?" I grabbed a rail as the train started, the tingling now pointing me straight south, in the direction the tracks would take us.

"That makes you an accomplice to nobly saving koi from impure water."

"You're an interesting person, Duncan."

"As we've established."

The train didn't travel far before the tingling in my chest intensified, wanting me to turn east.

"He might have gotten off at the next stop," I said.

"The potion can tell that?"

"My esophagus thinks so."

"It's amusing that you believe *I'm* the interesting one."

"Drinking weird potions tends to elevate one's quirkiness level." I headed for the door as the train slowed.

Duncan followed me out onto the platform and across a street heading east. It lacked a sidewalk and headed straight into a residential neighborhood with small ramblers that had been built in the mid-fifties. I thought of the convenience-store owners, Minato and Mayumi. Minato had shown me a photo of his house, and it had looked similar to these.

The tingling grew warmer, as if signaling that we were close.

"I expected their hideout to be in a box under a freeway or maybe a seedy motel," I said, "not a house in a normal-looking neighborhood."

"That one has overgrown grass and numerous cars on the lawn." Duncan pointed to a house across the street and around a corner that we were approaching. "Oh, and look at all the junk on the porch. Is that an old fridge?"

I snorted. "Those are signs of a hoarder, not a criminal."

"Are you sure? Those motorcycle thugs spend their evenings victimizing innocent people and vehicles in car parks. That may indicate a lack of time to devote to straightening and decluttering."

I was tempted to snort again, but my tingling chest *did* want us to angle around that corner, and... Was that a motorcycle under a tarp on the cracked, weed-choked driveway? On either side, fallen leaves that hadn't been tidied this past autumn remained, soggy among the yellow grass.

"That actually might be the place," I admitted.

"Naturally."

A curtain in the front window stirred.

"Someone's home." I thought about continuing past, pretending we were random pedestrians out for a walk, but I'd run into that guy enough times by now that he would recognize me. "Let's say hi."

"Hi, and have you seen a priceless sword from the Old World?"

"Sounds like a good greeting to me."

We crossed the street, heading toward the house, but a car roared out of nowhere and sped toward us. Duncan and I hustled into the driveway to avoid it, but it turned, tires squealing. If we hadn't sprung into the knee-high yellow grass, it would have struck us before braking.

The driver jumped out, holding a gun. At the same time, the house's back door banged open. My esophagus told me that my target had been responsible—and he was on the move.

"Keep that one from escaping." Duncan waved toward the backyard, then sprang onto the hood of the car and leaped for the gunman.

My first inclination was to stay at his side and help him, but then my target would escape. He was the whole reason I'd quaffed the awful potion.

I ran around the side of the house, leaped through a broken gate, and spotted the black-leather-wearing thug climbing a mildew-covered wood fence. The old boards quaked under his weight.

I sprinted toward him, a new tingle creeping into my body as adrenaline threatened to bring out the wolf. The thug reached the top of the fence, but I ran across the yard and leaped and grabbed his jacket before he could scramble to the other side. Summoning not-entirely-human strength, I yanked him back to the ground.

A gunshot thundered in the driveway out front.

Though worried about Duncan, I focused on my target as the big, bearded man lunged to his feet and threw a punch at me. Even though I lacked a lot of fighting experience beyond the six swordsmanship lessons, I had greater speed than a normal human and dodged the blow without trouble. I jumped in and gripped the man's shoulders. Before he could swing at me again, I drove my knee into his crotch.

Roaring, he tried to headbutt me. I released him, leaped back, and slammed the heel of my palm into his face. The cartilage of his nose crunched, and that dazed him. Eyes watering, the next punch he threw would have gone wild even if I hadn't dodged it. Unlike Radomir's brutes, this guy wasn't enhanced in any way, so no magic aided him.

I pushed him up against the fence.

"Tell me where my sword is, or I'll turn wolf and finish you off," I growled, certain that he knew by now that I had the power to do that.

"Don't know nothing about that." Through watering eyes, he glanced toward the back of the house.

Did he have more allies inside? A thump and a bang came from the front. I hoped that meant Duncan was dealing with the crazy driver—and anyone else who wanted to help this guy escape.

"Let go of me, bitch," the guy snarled, trying to heave me away.

I sank in, keeping him pinned. "Where are they keeping the sword? And who has it? Did they sell it, or do they still have it?"

Too bad I didn't sense any magic in the house. It would have been nice if this had led me to the invaluable sword, but I didn't detect anything out of the ordinary in the area.

My opponent jerked his face forward, again trying to headbutt me. I'd been ready for it and pulled back enough to avoid the contact, but he managed to get his hands on me and heft me into the air. Shit. I was strong, but I wasn't heavy.

I kicked at him. This time, he guarded his balls. He whirled and pinned *me* against the fence. I clipped him on the jaw with a punch, but I lacked leverage in this position, and the blow didn't hurt him much. He pulled me toward him, then slammed me against the fence, and my breath whooshed out.

My blood heated, magic surging through my limbs, my senses pricking with power. Since I was in trouble, I didn't try to tamp down the wolf. I wouldn't be able to question the man in that form, but the questioning wasn't going well anyway.

I squirmed, shoving at him, wanting to get away before changing since I would be vulnerable for the seconds that the transformation took. My phone flew out of my pocket.

My foe leaned in, trying to use his body to crush me to the fence. I hadn't yet changed, but I snarled and bit him on the ear. He screamed and let me go.

When I dropped, I landed on all fours. My body morphed, my clothes disappearing, and my hands and feet became paws. The scents of the grassy lawn and my sweating opponent flooded my nostrils, and the world sharpened around me, my foe growing less daunting. I crouched, muscles coiling.

Eyes wide, the human swore and backed up.

"Fendar, get out here!" he yelled.

A crash came from inside the house, and I paused. Was that my werewolf ally? I sensed him not far from here.

The thug in front of me grabbed a shovel and hefted it. I charged at him.

He swung the rusty blade at my head, but I dodged and snapped. With my jaws, I caught the wooden handle, crunched it in half, and tore the remains from his grip. Leaping in close, I snapped at my foe through his clothing, fangs sinking into the flesh of his hip.

The man cried out as he spun away. He attempted to run into the house, but I surged after him and sprang. I landed on his back and bore him to the ground.

Since the back of his neck was exposed, I could have killed him. But I vaguely remembered that in my other form I had wanted answers from him. He needed to remain alive. But when I'd questioned him, he hadn't provided the information I sought. If I wounded him badly enough would he be more accommodating?

Before I could find out, the roar of a vehicle engine came from the street out front. Something on the far side of the house shattered. A window?

"Look out!" a man shouted.

That was my ally, Duncan, still in his human form.

In the backyard, I paused, but I didn't know what his warning implied I should do. Underneath my paws, the man tried to squirm away. I lowered my jaws to the back of his neck, stilling him with sharp teeth on his flesh and my hot wolf breath.

He squawked in alarm.

"We didn't want to take it, okay?" he blurted. "We just want you to leave our turf alone. We don't care about your stuff. But the old guy told us to take it."

As a wolf, I struggled to grasp the significance of the words. The grunt I made might have had a querying tone, and the man must have interpreted it as a prompt for more information.

"No, not the sword, but the thing we couldn't find. The box with the wolf on it. That's what the old guy wanted. We—"

A great boom sounded in the house, and the back wall blew outward.

Wood and siding struck me, sending me rolling. Before I could find my feet, a huge white cylinder flew out of the house and slammed into me. Pain erupted as it knocked me all the way to and *through* the fence.

An inferno of fire roared through the roof as I tumbled into the yard of the house behind the broken fence. Flaming boards and shingles hit the ground, some striking me, singeing my fur.

When I tried to rise, sharp stabs of pain came from my ribs, and one of my legs wouldn't support my weight. I collapsed onto the yellow grass, whimpering as fire rained down all around me.

6

THE ENTIRE NEIGHBORHOOD DIDN'T CATCH FIRE, BUT THE HUMAN abode burned spectacularly. As people in nearby dwellings came out, I forced myself to my paws, my forelimb painful and my ribs cracked. Numerous lesser injuries aggravated me, spots where fire had burned through my fur.

Before limping out of the yard, I had the presence of mind to peer through the broken fence to see if any of my clothes had survived the change. If I took my human form again, I would need them.

Unfortunately, they had disappeared into the ether. A glint in the smoldering grass caught my eye. The paw-sized device that I so often used as a human. Knowing it held importance, I plucked it up and carried it away.

Aware of people gathering out front, I departed through the broken fence behind the human abode. Sticking to the yards, I traveled several dwellings away before veering toward the street. I wished to check on my ally.

I could sense him and that he still lived, but he was moving slowly away from the flaming house. Had he also been injured?

Severely burned? He'd been closer than I to the origins of that great destructive boom.

Between trees in front of another human domicile, one in which nobody seemed to be present, I spotted my ally. He had also changed, taking the form of a wolf rather than the two-legs, and he carried his jacket in his mouth.

Unlike me, he'd had the wherewithal to remove at least some of his clothing before changing. Also, unlike me, he wasn't limping. He hadn't escaped unscathed though. Blood matted his salt-and-pepper fur, and his movements were stiff. Further, much of his right side was charred, fur burned away, revealing blistered skin. The medallion that he'd worn under his shirt as a human, an artifact that belonged to my pack, had shifted along with him and hung around his neck. It glowed faintly, bathing him with its magic.

As quickly as my injured forelimb allowed, I hurried toward him. We met under the trees and slumped against each other.

Sirens wailed, coming from the direction of the great vehicle passageway. Our pointed ears flickered with displeasure as the noise increased, the source coming closer.

The glow of the medallion intensified, wrapping around me as well as Duncan. Though we were several yards away from the burning home, and most of the human observers watched the flames from the street out front of it, I worried the glow would attract notice. Perhaps thinking the same, Duncan backed toward evergreen bushes at the side of the property. Together, we found camouflage behind the leaves.

The medallion did more than glow. As it washed over us, the magic brought warmth that suffused my body. Though I doubted it could instantly heal our wounds, some of the pain lessened.

Duncan's wolf magic faded before mine, and he crouched as a human beside me, naked except for the medallion. Like many other items with power, it did not fall away during the change, instead staying with its possessor.

"That was a hell of an explosion." Gingerly, Duncan touched his side. As it had been in his wolf form, his skin was blistered and charred. "Did you see who threw the bomb?"

Understanding that he wanted to speak as humans did, I willed my wolf magic to fade. It would be easier to walk, anyway, since I only needed the back legs in that form. Nudity would be a problem, unfortunately. Humans had such strange conventions.

"I *did* in case you were wondering." Duncan grimaced. "Not in time to get out of the house and completely out of the way, but when I saw that familiar armored SUV roll up..."

The pain didn't go away with the change. If anything, it intensified after my body morphed, a reminder that humans weren't as tough as wolves.

When I crouched naked in the bushes beside Duncan, he repeated his last words. They had much more meaning to my human mind.

"*Radomir's* armored SUV?" I asked.

"Quite. I hadn't suspected that he had anything to do with the local brutes."

I started to nod in agreement but remembered the magical hand device that one thug had used on me the last time I'd defended my parking lot. I also struggled to recall the words of the man we'd tracked down, those he'd spat out when I'd stood over him as a wolf.

"The old guy."

Yes, he'd said that.

Duncan looked over, his eyebrows rising.

"The man we followed here said a few things before the explosion, that an *old guy* had ordered his gang to rob me. I think... they were supposed to get the wolf case, not necessarily the sword."

"That could have referred to either Radomir or Abrams."

"They're working together. It hardly matters."

"True," Duncan said. "Radomir would be the more likely to recruit local people. Abrams isn't from here, after all. Though I don't know how long he's been in the area."

"Maybe Radomir bartered some magical tools, a prize for the thugs if they were willing to steal from me. As long as they were harassing me anyway, why not add some theft into the mix?"

"The tools were probably meant to help them get what Radomir wants, not as a permanent gift."

"Either way, I'm going to consider them more dangerous now." I rose, cradling my arm to my torso and wondering if I needed to see a doctor for a splint. With luck, my wolf magic and whatever the medallion had done would help my arm heal soon. "Was Radomir the one driving the SUV? How would he have known we were hunting one of these guys? And why would he care, anyway?"

"I don't think it was him, just his vehicle. He lets his hired hands drive it from time to time."

"Such as when he needs someone rammed in the rear end and sent hurtling into the trees?" Fortunately, I'd managed to avoid that fate, but I felt resentment on behalf of my damaged truck.

"Yes. As to how he knew we were chasing that bloke, he might have glimpsed us or had someone at the train station keeping an eye out." Duncan shrugged. "A lookout could have called Radomir's men. Or maybe Radomir himself. He's been in the area recently, as we well know."

"Very recently. Maybe he and Abrams are lurking full-time in Shoreline now while they make fake offers on the apartment complex. We need to get back there before they try something else." I straightened, determined to leave before the police arrived and found us loitering.

"Our nudity could be a problem on the return trip." Duncan picked up his jacket. He, at least, wouldn't have to navigate Shoreline in daylight stark naked. "Does that city train of yours have regulations about clothing requirements?"

"Yeah, but they have regulations about using stolen koi-pond coins, too, and that didn't stop us before."

"I entreat you to research coin toxicity and fish. I assure you, you'll learn that my actions were heroic." Duncan handed me his jacket, nodding for me to put it on.

I sighed, appreciating his solicitude, though it annoyed me that I hadn't thought to shuck my own clothing. "Thank you. You *are* heroic."

"Of course. But you are the one with contacts in the area. Perhaps you could call someone to pick us up."

"Afraid of being arrested for nudity?"

"As we've discussed before, Americans are terribly repressed in that area."

I picked up my phone, glad I'd thought to grab it as a wolf, even if I had to rub saliva off the screen. "The problem with a lack of pockets," I murmured, pulling up Bolin's contact information. "I'm not sure what to do next about our problems, Duncan. We can't hunt down and kill Radomir and Abrams in the dark of night, can we?"

Maybe I shouldn't have sounded wistful when I asked that.

"Not without locating them first. Does your esophagus have any insights into their location?"

"No, my esophagus is as battered and burned as the rest of me and may not have insights on anything for a while."

"Not even chocolate?" Duncan leaned over, poked into one of the jacket pockets, and withdrew a few espresso beans covered in half-melted speckled white chocolate, then offered them to me.

I leaned on him, glad to have him at my side. I almost said something mushy and oozing with feelings of warmth and gratitude, but then I remembered my conversation with Abrams, that Duncan might be dying. I *really* didn't know what to do next.

7
***

Bolin kept his eyes toward the road as he drove us to Sylvan Serenity, me in the passenger seat, Duncan in the back. Bolin hadn't mentioned the fire engines or the smoldering house when he'd picked us up, and, after gaping at our nudity, had pointedly avoided looking at us. That hadn't kept him from grimacing when we sat our bare butts on the fancy leather of his Mercedes SUV. We *were* sooty, bloody, and sweaty, so I couldn't blame him. I would have objected to such butts on my weathered vinyl truck seats.

"Thanks for getting us," I said for the second time. "Even though I've lived in the same area for years—decades—and made a number of friends in the years the boys were in school... there are precious few people I can call for a ride when I've lost all my clothes."

"Repressed," Duncan said again.

"*That's* not why. But I would feel compelled to explain."

"You didn't explain anything to your intern," Duncan said.

I looked at Bolin. Still focused on the road, he did not look back.

"I think he prefers it when I don't," I said.

"Correct," Bolin said.

"Any news on the apartment sale?" I asked to change the subject, though we fortunately did not have a long drive back.

"My mom sent over a list of things that she and Dad would like done in the next week or so, ideally before the inspection that will precede the sale."

"The sale that's a ruse and won't happen? Send me the list." I didn't believe for a second that an actual sale would come out of Abrams and Radomir's offer, whether on paper or not, but someone would buy the place eventually. Again, I hoped my wounds healed quickly, especially the throbbing arm and ribs. I refused to ask for any time off work.

Bolin opened his mouth, presumably to continue the conversation, but we'd pulled into the lot and he blurted, "Is that Jasmine's car?"

"The little hatchback?" I leaned forward, spotting it. "Yes. Maybe her father was able to look up that license plate."

That probably wasn't what had brought her. She could have texted me the address if that was all that was up.

"I didn't think she'd come here so soon." Bolin sounded excited but also nervous, and he rushed to scrape his fingers through his hair and look at himself in the rearview mirror.

"Did *you* invite her over?" I asked.

"Yeah. I want to ask her on a date, and I thought it might go better if I do it in person."

"Because she'll be less likely to reject you to your face?"

"That's what I'm hoping. But I said... Uhm, I might have gotten her to come by using... implying... Well, it's not really a false pretense. It's *true*." On that vague note, Bolin parked and turned off the car.

Jasmine stood by the staff spots and waved at us. Bolin slid out.

I looked into the back seat, wondering how much the car doors blocked Duncan's nudity from outside viewers. And mine for that matter. I wore his jacket but remained naked from the waist down. And Duncan might as well have been Michelangelo's *David* back there.

Jasmine wouldn't be surprised or perturbed by our states, but numerous tenants were coming and going from the parking lot. We would need an opportune moment to head to my apartment or Duncan's van.

"Hi, Bolin," Jasmine said. "How come you couldn't tell me about the networking opportunity over the phone?"

Ah, that was the false pretense.

"Because of Luna." Bolin pointed at me.

I rolled down the window, curious how I would play into him asking for a date. Chilly air swept in, curling around my bare legs.

"She may also be interested in going to a networking event," Bolin said. "In case... Well, the buyers who put in the offer didn't appear eager to work with her, so she may also be looking for new employment soon."

"Alas, true," I murmured.

"You don't want to work for Radomir anyway," Duncan said from the back seat. "He's a tyrant and makes you drink unpalatable potions."

"I drank an unpalatable potion for *you*."

"Not because you work for me and I ordered it. It was voluntary, presumably because you pined for me in my absence and were thus moved to great sacrifice. You had to ensure I would return to your life."

"I was pining for you," I said.

"I assumed."

"I did suggest that Luna and I could go networking together." Jasmine nodded at me. "Then we could talk each other up."

"An excellent idea," Bolin said.

I wanted to gag, more at the idea of *networking* than going somewhere with Jasmine and talking her up. The thought of job hunting after so many years of not needing to... It filled me with greater anxiety than battling werewolves or facing rifles loaded with silver bullets.

"My parents let me know about an exclusive gathering at the private residence of a real estate mogul in Bellevue this Friday. There will be a lot of well-to-do industry people there, talking about new developments being planned for the area. Even though the market has slowed down, those in the top echelon tend to do well in any environment. I'm sure some of them will have positions in need of filling." Bolin extended his hand toward Jasmine. "I could get you on the guest list if you would be interested in going." After only a slight pause, he remembered me and waved in my direction. "Both of you."

I wondered when in his plans came the part where he would ask Jasmine on a date.

"That does sound like the kind of event my mom would like me to go to." The face Jasmine made suggested she felt the same about networking as I did.

"It's in a penthouse with a big balcony and a view of the lake," Bolin said. "I understand you can see all the way to the Olympic Mountains. There'll be a private chef handling the refreshments and a bartender too."

"Are people more likely to hire you after their stomachs are full and they're tipsy?" I asked.

"If they're in a jovial mood, I would think so." Bolin nodded.

Jasmine bit her lip.

Bolin leaned forward, watching her face. Hoping she would go to the party, get a job, and thus be grateful to him? Or was it more than that?

"Are you going to the event, Bolin?" I asked on a hunch. Maybe this *was* the date he had in mind.

"Most likely, yes. My parents are going, and they want me to meet some of their colleagues. I've met a lot of them already, of course, but less in a work-colleague capacity and more as..."

"Your parents' goofy kid?" I guessed.

Bolin grimaced. "One of their colleagues hasn't seen me since she stepped on my LEGOs at a summer barbecue my parents hosted several years back. Anyway, there's no pressure. You don't have to come." He'd turned back to Jasmine. "It's just that I heard you were looking for a job in the industry, and this could be a good opportunity to meet people who might be hiring. For both of you." Only slightly belatedly, he waved toward me again.

"Am I invited too?" Duncan asked dryly.

Bolin blinked at him. "You're... naked."

"I guess I'm not invited," Duncan told me.

"Nudity isn't considered highbrow in America," I said.

"Repressed," he said again.

Jasmine looked toward Duncan's window, but, as I'd expected, didn't bat an eye at his nudity. She could probably tell I wasn't wearing anything under the jacket either.

"You said it's Friday night?" Jasmine asked Bolin.

"Yes. Do you want me to pick you both up?" He pointed to include me.

"I'll pass on networking events until I know for sure if I'm out of a job." I figured Bolin would appreciate it if I gave him an excuse to take Jasmine without a chaperone.

But he looked at me without relief. In fact, his eyes were oddly intent. "You might want to reconsider, Luna."

"A night of making small-talk with rich real estate developers?" I wrinkled my nose. "I'd rather spend the next week hugging my heating pad, eating chocolates, and remembering how to breathe without pain." I touched my tender ribs, doubting I would have the opportunity to live that fantasy. My arm twinged. I needed to end this chat and find my first-aid kit—if not a number for a doctor.

"Ivan MacGregor is hosting the event."

I tried to remember the name and why it would be significant.

"The guy the newspaper mentioned," Bolin added.

"Oh, because he was robbed of a wolf bracelet?"

He nodded.

I *had* debated on trying to find a way to question that man. I scratched my jaw and looked back at Duncan. He hadn't been there when I'd read that article, and he merely raised his eyebrows.

It wasn't as if I had any better leads. The thug who might have known where my sword was had gotten away, Radomir and Abrams moved hideouts more often than gophers avoiding red-tailed hawks, and I would need a few days of sedate activities while my battered body healed.

"Maybe I will go," I told Bolin. "Who can pass up a shindig with an open bar?"

"Shindig," he mouthed.

Presumably, it wasn't a word Gen-Zers used with any frequency.

"Yeah, do you know the origins and how to spell it?"

"I can *spell* it. I... may need to research the origins. That was used less often than you might think in spelling bees."

"I finally stymied my young intern," I told Duncan.

"It's from the Scottish game *shinty*, I believe," he said.

"I'll research it," Bolin said firmly.

"That means he doesn't trust you as a resource," I said to Duncan.

Duncan touched a hand to his bare chest. "I've traveled the world and read thousands of books."

"Yeah, but you're naked. That invalidates a lot."

"Why would my dress state subtract from my wisdom? This is such a *strange* country."

"Are you going to call it repressed again?"

"Hourly, yes."

8

By the evening of the networking event, my ribs and my arm weren't bothering me as much. The pain had eased from excruciating to merely sore, and I could breathe without twinges of agony. I did still have bandages wrapped around my torso to support what had likely been broken ribs.

Thank the moon for the regenerative power of the werewolf—and that Radomir hadn't directed any thugs to my door these past couple of days. He *had* sent an appraiser over, as if he were a legitimate buyer. I still couldn't believe he wanted the place. Why was he going through such an elaborate charade?

"What a week," I said from the passenger seat of Jasmine's hatchback on the way to Bellevue with her.

Grimacing, I tugged at the collar of my mock turtleneck, one of a handful of items I owned that qualified as "dress clothing." They'd all been purchased in another decade. They hadn't been comfortable then, and they weren't comfortable now. At least they still fit, though I wasn't as svelte and sleek as I had been in my youth. Naturally, I blamed that on childbirth twenty years ago rather than my dark-chocolate addiction.

Jasmine glanced at me. "It'll be fine."

"Do I look nervous?"

"Yup."

She wore a flowing emerald-green tunic and khaki trousers that looked fashionable, at least to my untrained eye. I kept up on the latest trends in paint, flooring, and window coverings but paid less attention to what people wore.

"Do you ever get phantom tail twitches?" Jasmine asked.

"What is that?"

"When you're a human but you feel like you're sitting on your tail or what you're wearing is irritating it."

"I don't think so. I just get twitchy in general when I'm out of my element."

"Tell me about it," Jasmine said. "When people waste my time with small talk, I get urges to bite them."

"Really? You always seem less... *lupine* than a lot of the family. You have equanimity."

"Wolves can't have equanimity?"

"Since I stopped taking the sublimation potions, I've struggled to keep my alter ego from springing out and pouncing on people."

"Cats pounce. Wolves maim and mutilate."

"That doesn't sound as elegant."

"You've *met* the family, right?"

I snorted. Yes. We could be graceful during the hunt, but we did trend a touch brutish. More so than non-magical wolves in the wilds. *They* had equanimity.

"Almost there." Jasmine pointed at the map on her phone.

Her car didn't have a screen to tie into it, but neither did my truck. I was used to modest amenities when it came to transportation. And, unlike my truck, both of her fenders were attached.

"This is in an expensive part of town." Jasmine eyed the highrises as we drove past.

"I don't think Bellevue has any *inexpensive* parts."

"Well, there are places where the median home price is less than others."

"So, under a million dollars?"

"Not *that* much less." Jasmine smirked. "It's why I'll probably end up with a condo in Everett instead. The kind that overlooks the freeway or an alley. Probably an alley *next* to a freeway. That's if I'm lucky enough to find something. Home ownership isn't exactly easy to swing in the Seattle area on a single person's income. I might have to move into one of your apartments and rent for a while."

"They won't be my apartments for long."

I didn't point out that being the property manager didn't give me a claim on ownership. She knew that.

"That's a bummer. You've kept them up really well."

"Thank you." Since we were almost there, I delved into my purse and sifted through my budgeting envelopes. I pulled a few bills out of the one labeled GAS and tucked them into one of the drink holders.

"Is that a tip for good driving?"

"I'm chipping in for gas money."

"Since I'm currently unemployed, I'm not going to be too proud to take it."

"Good."

At a stoplight, Jasmine slipped the bills into her purse. "The next owners won't know what to do if your apartment complex gets overrun with werewolves."

"Fewer landlords than you'd think know what to do in that circumstance."

"I know for a fact that deer repellent doesn't work on werewolves. Dad sprayed his fruit trees with the stuff, and, the first time Emilio and Alessio visited, they headed straight to the backyard. I think Emilio licked a leaf."

"Must have dried blood in the mix. I've tried all the various

repellents to keep rabbits from noshing on the pansies and petu-
nias I plant around the grounds in the spring. I finally gave up and
hung them in baskets instead of putting them in the ground."

"This is a weird conversation for carnivores to have."

"I'm not the one with a relative growing fruit trees."

"Dad produces apple and pear cider with his fruit. Making
booze appeals to carnivores as well as normies." Jasmine nodded
toward a turn ahead. We were passing more tall modern buildings,
one with walls appearing to be made entirely of glass, the western
side reflecting the setting sun. "It's just around the corner."

Hopefully, taking this time away from figuring out what
Radomir and Abrams were up to wouldn't prove a mistake.
Duncan had said he would keep an eye on Sylvan Serenity in case
any trouble came by this evening, and the police patrol car was
back in the street near the lot.

Such deterrents might keep the tenants' vehicles from being
vandalized, but they wouldn't get me any closer to figuring out
how to help Duncan or what Radomir and Abrams were up to.

We pulled into a parking lot full of sporty Porsches, convert-
ible BMWs, and, for the more ruggedly-inclined luxury auto
buyer, Bentley and Rolls-Royce SUVs. I spotted a similar model G-
Wagon to what Bolin had but in a different color. It gleamed from
a recent detail and lacked bird droppings of any kind.

At least I didn't see any armored SUVs. I wouldn't put it past
Radomir to have figured out I was coming here so he could send
his thugs to try again to kill me.

"Bolin's car would fit in here more than mine." Jasmine waved
at a valet who was eyeing us like we were potential thieves. "Too
bad he was driving his parents. He could have given us a ride."

"He offered to bring us."

"Yeah, but we might have ended up squeezed in the back with
his mom and dad. That would have been weird."

If Jasmine had accepted his offer, he probably would have

shown up without his mom and dad. I smirked as I imagined him punting his parents out and telling them to get an Uber as he patted the passenger seat to invite Jasmine in.

"I wasn't sure about riding with him regardless." She glanced at me as she bypassed the valet and drove toward empty spots at the back of the lot. "I get the vibe that he wants to ask me out."

"That might be an accurate vibe. You're not interested?" I hadn't asked that before. Maybe I should have instead of helping Bolin with his selection of rap music with which to serenade her.

"He's... not horrible looking."

"Don't say that within his hearing, or he'll have tremendous hope of his pursuit being fruitful."

Jasmine made a face. "It's just that he's pretty geeky. Like if he were a wolf, he'd be an omega. It might be like dating my dad."

"Your dad seems like a good guy. He keeps doing research for me for free, and he makes his own hard cider."

"He *is* a good guy. You know, for my mom. For women who want to be married and have a stable life. I'm more into the alphas and betas. And I want someone *exciting*."

"Bolin's life has gotten pretty exciting since he started working for me."

Jasmine laughed. "I don't doubt *that*. My last few weeks have been pretty interesting too."

She parked and grabbed a gem-studded green purse that went with her outfit, wisely adding a fur-trimmed jacket as well. Despite the atypical sun we'd had today, the light—and warmth—it emitted this time of year were wan, and it was already setting.

Hoping I wouldn't have any urges to change during the party —the networking event—I grabbed a jacket of my own. Even if I didn't adore my dress clothes, I also didn't want to pay to replace them if something prompted me to get furry. Curling a lip, I tugged at the turtleneck collar again.

A doorman let us in without asking for proof of invitations, and we passed through a marble-tiled lobby with fancy fountains and chandeliers, each probably costing more than the alley-adjacent condominiums Jasmine had mentioned.

A uniformed elevator operator with the build of a bouncer asked to see our invitations. An email that Bolin had forwarded from his parents did the job, though someone else with a gilded envelope entered with us. The operator pressed a button to send us toward the penthouse before stepping out.

"I guess this is where you work if robots and automation make your job obsolete," Jasmine murmured.

"I shouldn't have to worry about that for a while. I haven't seen many robots capable of replacing toilets yet."

The woman in the elevator looked over at us. Her expression wasn't exactly scandalized, but I did get the vibe that this wasn't the kind of shindig where one brought up such pedestrian items as toilets. Considering it was for real estate people, that struck me as odd. Surely, some of them had replaced bathroom fixtures as they made their way up in the world.

When the doors opened, the woman stepped out quickly, waving to acquaintances and hurrying away from us. The foyer up here was almost as fancy as the one downstairs, and only four doors marked units on the floor, one standing open.

"I don't think I'm going to fit in here." As we entered, I eyed servers with trays of one-bite appetizers and sparkling beverages in crystal glasses. The help was dressed nicer than I was, making me wonder if this was a more formal affair than Bolin had led me to believe.

"Probably not, but it's a cool view." Jasmine waved to floor-to-ceiling windows that overlooked Lake Washington in the distance. Another uniformed doorman stood at the balcony access point, allowing guests to come and go. Outside, patio heaters glowed warmly for those interested in mingling in the evening air. "*Much* cooler than any condo I'll ever be able to afford." She sighed longingly.

"The alley freeway in Everett isn't the view of your dreams?"

"It'll be okay for a starter home. Anything to be independent and stop feeling like I'm mooching off my parents."

"Maybe you should rethink your interest in Bolin," I said, though I approved that she didn't seem to find him more appealing because he came from money.

"Does he have a penthouse?"

"I'm not sure. I just know his car is expensive and coddled."

"*Most* guys' cars are coddled."

"Yeah, but how many men do you know who carry around portable blow-up garages for theirs?"

"Not many. He *was* pretty good in a fight," Jasmine admitted. "He threw bath bombs everywhere."

"Orbs of Entanglement."

"Yeah, that's what he called them, but they looked like the swirly chamomile-and-green-tea balls I toss in the tub for a relaxing soak."

"I think he makes them himself." I wiggled my fingers to indicate *with magical power* rather than that he had a bath-bomb press.

"Hm." She led off into the crowd, more of a determined walk than a mingle.

I doubted Jasmine was a natural networker either.

"Do you know what the guy you want to talk to looks like?" she asked. "He's the host, right? He shouldn't be too hard to find."

"Yes, I looked him up and got a photo off his LinkedIn." I took my phone out to show her a fifty-something guy wearing a denim shirt and cowboy hat.

"Is he from Bellevue or Texas?"

"Yelm, actually. According to his bio, he got his start working on ranches down there while fixing up his first properties."

"Huh. He probably won't be too hoity-toity then. Yelm isn't

exactly... Shoot, I don't even know where that is exactly. South of Olympia, right?"

"More or less." I scanned the crowd, looking for the man. "It's larger than Deming and Maple Falls."

Jasmine snorted. "*That* doesn't say much."

A couple of young women walked past, their arms linked to older men. Looking like the definition of *trophy wives*, they sniffed at me and my mock turtleneck. What did it say about me that I would rather have spent an evening fighting burly heavies hopped up on potions?

"Is Bolin *sure* this is a party for people in the real estate industry?" I asked. "Most of the developers and investors I've met, at least in the Seattle area, were more down-to-earth than this."

"These guests do have a vibe of uselessness, don't they?" Despite taking a dig at the people here, Jasmine smiled when a server brought over a tray and offered us drinks.

Feeling the need for social lubrication, I accepted a glass of champagne.

"Do you have any mocktails?" Jasmine asked. "I'm the driver."

"Yes, ma'am. I'll see what I can find." The male server, who wasn't much older than she, smiled warmly at her before walking off.

I decided it would be petty to be envious of my niece's youth and radiant beauty.

"The real-estate networking events that my mom goes to would be more your style, I think," Jasmine said. "She gives talks at monthly meetups at a pizzeria/bowling alley in the 'burbs. The group can get the side room there for free as long as they order a few pizzas and sodas. The owners are kind of stingy about drink refills, though, and sometimes your conversations get drowned out by pins in the closest lane being knocked down."

"It does sound like a place where I'd be more comfortable."

"Want me to get you an invite to the next meeting? You'd fit in.

These rich guys are an anomaly." Jasmine waved to encompass the spacious penthouse. "Most real estate investors that my mom works with drive dumpier cars than their tenants, house hack, and do their own repairs and property management, just like you. They put every penny into saving for their next rental. It's not until they've been in the game for a couple of decades that anyone might consider them rich."

"Sign me up."

The server returned with two offerings for Jasmine, one smelling of mint and the other of citrus bitters. As she selected the latter and took a sip, I skimmed the crowd for the face I'd looked up. Ivan MacGregor. Though Jasmine had come to further her career prospects, I only wanted to speak with him about his stolen wolf bracelet.

Ah, there he was.

Tonight, he wore a Seahawks cap rather than the cowboy hat, but with jeans and a flannel shirt, he was much more dressed-down than his guests. He meandered through the gathering, greeting everyone while giving shoulder thumps to the men and polite hand clasps to the women. Making sure everyone was enjoying themselves?

"I'm going to introduce myself," I told Jasmine, who was chatting with the server about the increasing popularity of *mocktails* instead of finding someone who might give her a job.

She lifted a hand in acknowledgment.

As I headed toward Ivan, he walked up to an elegant woman in her late thirties who stood near a cheerfully blazing gas fireplace. She'd brought a girl of seven or eight, her daughter presumably, who was assiduously tapping away on her phone.

I paused, startled. Both mother and daughter had a feral vibe. A *lupine* vibe.

I wasn't the only werewolf at the party.

9

THE MOM WITH THE LUPINE VIBE LOOKED IN MY DIRECTION, OUR EYES locking. She squinted, then frowned. Picking up *my* feral vibe? Worse, she tapped Ivan on the shoulder and pointed at me.

"Really?" he asked, turning in my direction.

The woman nodded. Now, they both squinted at me, suspicion in their eyes.

I froze, debating between continuing forward to talk to them and springing toward the elevator to flee. But I wasn't, I told myself, doing anything wrong. I had an invitation to the party.

That didn't keep me from breaking out in a sweat when they walked toward me, the mom gripping her daughter's hand. The girl complained and waved her phone, a game open on the screen. But when she noticed me, she lowered it and grew quiet.

"Good evening," Ivan said. "May I get you a drink refill?" He waved to my glass, which I'd barely sipped, then lowered his voice to add, "Or something to eat? A raw steak perhaps?"

The woman's eyebrows didn't so much as twitch. She eyed me up and down, as if she thought we might fight later and wanted to gauge my strengths and weaknesses.

I *hoped* that wouldn't be necessary. I couldn't imagine that turning furry in the middle of a cocktail party would help me get a new property-management job. If anything, I needed a kitchen faucet to spontaneously spring a leak, giving me the opportunity to fix it in front of everyone.

"I only eat raw food that I've hunted myself." I kept myself from glancing to the side to check on Jasmine. If the werewolf mom hadn't noticed my niece yet, I didn't want to draw attention to her.

"What's your favorite prey?" The woman had a sultry voice.

"Elk." I eyed her. "What's *yours*?"

"Javelina is delicious."

I blinked. Where was she hunting javelinas? "I haven't tried that before."

"It's a sweet, mild, pork-like meat. Javelinas are common in Arizona."

I didn't know what to make of the factoid until Ivan said, "My half-sister, Izzy, is visiting from Scottsdale." He tilted his head toward her. "I got her into real estate a few years ago, and now she owns more than two hundred units in the Phoenix metro area."

"I bet she doesn't have any trouble collecting rents," I said.

"I don't." The mom—Izzy—flashed her teeth, including canines as sharp as mine.

The kid looked back and forth between us.

"What brings you to my little event..." Ivan trailed off, prompting me for my name.

"Luna Valens."

"You haven't been here before, have you?" Ivan gave his sister a significant look.

Only then did I realize he might believe I'd had something to do with the theft. A werewolf might naturally be interested in werewolf artifacts, after all.

"I haven't, no. I work for the Sylvans." I looked around and was relieved to spot Rory and Kashvi stepping off the elevator with Bolin.

I lifted a hand toward them, but Bolin beelined straight for Jasmine without noticing me. Fortunately, Rory saw me and returned the wave. Some acquaintance of Kashvi's intercepted her and drew her off, but Rory walked over.

"Evening, Ivan, Luna. Bolin said you might come." He nodded to me before looking toward the host.

"This is my half-sister, Izzy," Ivan said to Rory. "Good of you to come. Davenport is pitching your property to his syndicate. You might be amused and also offended by what he sent out in his email."

"That it's at under-market rents, poorly maintained by uncaring and inexperienced management, and a candidate for an easy value-add resulting in a huge profit?" Rory asked dryly.

"It's also haunted, I understand."

Rory snorted. "Luna has been our property manager and on-site maintenance person for more than twenty years. It's a cash cow. If anything, new ownership may have trouble keeping it quite as profitable."

"Is she also the reason it's haunted?" Izzy twitched her eyebrows.

A touch of panic welled up in me as I realized this woman whom I'd never met—this *werewolf* from Scottsdale—could out me to my employers. I'd considered before that Rory might already know about the lupine aspect of his property manager, especially since he had paranormal blood himself, but he didn't radiate as much druidic power as his son, so it was possible he'd never detected my magical nature. And Kashvi... She was completely normal. I couldn't imagine her stern no-nonsense business acumen approving of something as mercurial as a were-wolf working for the family business.

"It's not haunted," I hurried to say. "Those are rumors started

by some of the tenants. They walk around at night with ghos-
tometers."

"But there *have* been incidents there." Ivan raised his
eyebrows. "People killed."

"It's near the freeway and not in the best neighborhood." A
bead of sweat slithered down my spine. "But the police are helping
out. There's been a patrol car there lately."

Rory looked at me. Maybe I should have shut up. This wasn't
the kind of *networking* I'd wanted to do here.

"I handle what I can myself," I added, feeling self-conscious
since others around us had stopped talking to look over. "When
thugs on motorcycles come by, I'm not above hurling the landscaping rocks at them to keep them from vandalizing my tenants'
cars."

Izzy surprised me by laughing. "I'll bet."

"Motorcycles, you say?" Ivan's eyes had sharpened. Had parking-lot footage here caught his thieves departing on Harleys?

The girl tugged on her mom's sleeve, pointed at Bolin, and
walked off in that direction. Great, the rest of my paranormal allies
were going to be outed as well.

"Davenport tends to email his people the same spiel no matter
how well-run a complex is," Ivan said. "He's better at gathering
money from his LPs than actually improving properties and giving
anyone great returns."

"I've noticed," Rory said.

"What brings your property manager here?" Ivan looked at
me, though he directed the question to Rory.

"She wants to start investing in real estate herself is what my
son said," Rory said, surprising me. Was that what Bolin had told
his parents to snag invitations for us? Maybe people fishing for
jobs weren't encouraged to come.

"Investing in what?" Izzy asked. "Suitable lairs for her pack?"

I was starting to dislike her. "I'm hoping to start with a four-plex so I can get a conventional thirty-year loan."

"You'll have plenty of experience with leasing and maintaining it." Rory gave me a friendly nod. "And keeping it secure."

I kept my face neutral, but was that an implication that he knew about my werewolf status? It made me uneasy. How many of the newspaper articles had he seen? The one that hypothesized a *wolf* might have killed those thugs?

"I do live there," I said. "It's important to watch out for your home."

"Indeed," Rory said.

"Security?" Ivan looked me up and down. "Because of your heritage? Or do you practice martial arts?"

"I... absolutely." I'd had those six lessons at the dojo, after all. "I'm becoming an expert on keeping apartments secure, and I have allies who can help me find those who do my tenants wrong."

At the least, Rue could give me dreadful-tasting potions to assist in that capacity.

"Oh?" Ivan's eyes sharpened with interest. "Like a skip tracer?"

He seemed to have gone from suspecting me to wanting to know more about my abilities for some other reason. Was he looking for someone to get his stolen artifact back? If only I could. But I'd yet to retrieve even my own sword.

"She probably tracks them through other means." Izzy touched the side of her nose.

"I can find people," I said, not going into my *means*. "I'm mostly the muscle, but I have an acquaintance who can make all manner of things that assist with the finding."

"The muscle?" Ivan asked with amusement, eyeing me again—specifically my five-foot-three inches and one-hundred-ten pounds, I had no doubt.

"Our businessman, Ed, has seen her carry one-piece toilets up flights of stairs," Rory said. "He remarked on it some time ago."

I didn't know if that was his way of backing up my assertion or letting me know he'd been aware for a while that I had paranormal attributes.

"Carrying *toilets*?" a woman whispered, catching the conversation as she and a friend passed. They wore enough gold and diamonds to make Mr. T sigh with envy. "Is she the plumber?"

"I don't know, but someone should tell her that mock turtlenecks are deserving of mockery."

They giggled as they continued on. I rolled my eyes. I'd come to a party of high-school cliques, not a real estate networking event. So far, I'd hardly heard anyone speaking of available properties, tired landlords, and capitalization rates.

"Could I consult with you on something, Ms. Valens, was it?" Ivan asked.

"One moment." Izzy gave me an edged smile and pulled her brother aside. No doubt to fill him in more deeply on my lupine nature—and what all that entailed.

"Don't listen to them." Jasmine appeared, stepping close enough to poke me in the arm, a new mocktail in her hand, this one colored Jello-green. "Turtlenecks are back in style this winter. Those girls aren't as trendy as they think they are."

Rory arched his eyebrows. Jasmine offered me a discreet thumbs-up. I didn't know if it was to encourage me to feel better about my fashion choices or because she approved of the high-powered people I was *networking* with. Too bad Izzy was about to get me kicked out.

"Evening, ma'am," Rory said to Jasmine.

I realized they probably hadn't met before.

"Mr. Sylvan, this is my niece, Jasmine Marino." Taking a cue from the earlier conversation, I didn't mention that she hoped to score a job. "She works in real estate financing."

"Here looking for clients?" Rory asked.

"I don't have my own lending business yet. I mostly help out my mom. And Luna." Jasmine smirked at me.

"She needs financing assistance?"

"She needs all *kinds* of assistance." Jasmine straightened my hem and flipped hair off my shoulder.

"I can imagine. I—" Rory noticed something across the room.

Bolin looked like he was in the middle of being grilled by Izzy's daughter. The girl had pulled over a chair to stand on so she was as tall as he. She was waving her arms and questioning him about who knew what. Meanwhile, Bolin was gesturing toward his father, trying to get his attention. When their gazes met, Bolin nodded and widened his eyes significantly toward Jasmine.

"Ah, you are *that* Jasmine," Rory said.

"What?" Jasmine stopped fixing my trendy outfit and lowered her arm.

"I can see the allure." Rory inclined his head politely toward her.

"The what?" Jasmine looked at me instead of Bolin, who was now trying to wave his father away from her, probably afraid Rory would do something to lower his chances of winning her favor.

Before Rory could answer, the siblings returned.

Izzy was scowling, but Ivan said, "Ms. Valens. I am more intrigued than ever to get your professional opinion on something."

"As a property manager?" Rory asked.

"As a security professional," Ivan said.

"What is it?" I asked before Rory could point out that I wasn't a *professional* in that area.

"Come this way, please."

Rory remained, likely deciding the invitation wasn't for him, but Jasmine trailed me as Ivan led us toward a closed door.

Before we reached it, Bolin veered in from the side, the daughter walking with him and asking him questions about druids and if he could change into a bear. She wasn't being quiet, and numerous people turned toward them with curious or puzzled expressions.

"Jasmine," Bolin whispered, "can you help me with something?"

He glanced at the girl.

"This isn't a good idea," Izzy whispered to her brother as they walked ahead of us. "Don't give her access to anything. She could come back and take everything you've got."

"She won't do that," Ivan replied. "I'm good at reading people. It's how I've negotiated so many successful deals."

"Oh, please. You lucked into getting into the market at the bottom of the crash, like everyone else here. You couldn't deal your way to a part-time gig at a convenience store."

"Have I mentioned how much your sisterly support means to me?"

"You called me up to the Pacific Northwest in the middle of its gray and dreary winter. And I *came*. How much more support do you want?"

Not answering, Ivan led me into a bedroom larger than my apartment. Bolin had successfully diverted Jasmine away. I didn't know whether to be concerned about being alone with these two or not.

In the bedroom, a gas fireplace blazed cheerily in front of a seating area separate from the king bedroom set that faced floor-to-ceiling windows overlooking the lake. Outside, it had grown too dark to see much of the water, but the city lights of Seattle were visible on the far shoreline.

"In here, Ms. Valens." Ivan stepped into a spacious closet, built-in mahogany shelves and cabinets lining the walls. Two posh leather chairs offered spots to sit to put on one's socks in the morning.

Before I could follow Ivan inside, Izzy grasped my forearm.

Her grip was strong, a testament to her lupine heritage, and her fingers dug in.

My hackles rose as I glared at her. "What's your problem?"

"My *problem* is that some wolf reeking of the Snohomish Savagers walked into my brother's party." Izzy squinted at me. "You're from that pack, aren't you?"

I tried to hide my surprise, not that she could tell about my heritage from my scent or aura but that she was familiar with the local pack. Wasn't she from Arizona? Or had she also grown up in Yelm?

"Yes. So?"

"You're *not* to be trusted. None of them are."

"What pack are *you* from?" I asked quietly.

She might have filled in her half-brother on my heritage, but he wasn't a werewolf, so I didn't want to confess anything in front of him. Someone like Ivan had the power to ruin my real estate ambitions—maybe *all* of my ambitions.

I glanced toward the bedroom door, thinking of pulling away and leaving. Finding out about Ivan's missing bracelet and if he knew more about who'd taken it wasn't *that* important.

"Before they departed, devastated by the loss of a prominent up-and-coming alpha, I belonged to the Cascade Crushers." Izzy stared me in the eye. "I've been in Arizona a long time, but I haven't forgotten about my pack or what prompted them to leave this area."

"Oh," I mouthed at the unexpected revelation.

Despite the gathering outside, it had grown silent in the bedroom. Inside the closet, Ivan knelt, touching a panel that slid up to reveal a safe, the side torched black, the door askew. Not focusing on us, he set about opening it, not with a fingerprint or keypad but a pry bar. The thieves must have warped the door when they'd broken into it.

"Raoul was my cousin." Izzy's fingers dug deeper into my arm. "He was a good kid, a lover, not a fighter, despite his power."

Yes, I'd often described him that way myself. The night we'd fought, when I'd lost myself to the savage wild instincts that always lurked, threatening to take over my body and deprive me of my rational mind... Raoul hadn't fought back as much as he could have. As he *should* have. If he had, he would have defeated me instead of the other way around.

"He was." I struggled for calm, but the wolf wanted to burst out of me. My body tensed, hating that a threat stood so close, her fingers presumptuously and painfully gripping my arm.

"I think I know who you are, what you did," Izzy said.

"I loved him."

"You *killed* him." Magic rippled around her, and she released me to step back. Would she shift into a wolf to attack me?

"There we go." Ivan stepped into the doorway of the closet. "Ms. Valens?"

I didn't want to tear my gaze from Izzy, not when she was on the verge of changing, when she radiated loathing as well as magic. She must have held this pain, this grudge, for more than twenty years. And for the first time, she saw the opportunity to act upon it.

"Yes?" Out of my peripheral vision, I could see Ivan looking expectantly at me.

"I'd like your opinion on a security matter. On a theft I recently suffered, in truth." Speaking in a calm, matter-of-fact voice, Ivan didn't notice that his sister was glaring daggers at me and on the verge of changing into a wolf. Of course, as a mundane human, he wouldn't sense the magic. He'd clearly been born to only one parent with lycanthropic blood. He was, like my sons, perfectly normal. "If you've a way to track down robbers, I could make it worth your while. Monetarily or by putting in a good word with whomever." He waved airily, as if either would be a simple matter and wouldn't bother him.

"I'll be happy to have a look."

Izzy *growled*. It was too low in her throat for her brother to hear, but she could spring at me at any moment.

This might be Ivan's home and party, but I doubted he had the power to stop her if she turned into a wolf. I would have to fight her, and then what? My senses told me I was probably stronger than she was—though they also suggested she was the kind of person to fight dirty and take advantage of distractions—but that didn't mean I would win. What if I lost my rational mind and killed her, right here in her brother's bedroom with a hundred people outside the door? A hundred potential witnesses? Hell, my employers were out there.

"Great," Ivan said. "In here, please. Step aside, Izzy, will you?"

She didn't, not until the bedroom door opened and her daughter peered inside. "Mom? Can druids change into bears? And would it be a *grizzly* bear? Or like a black bear?"

Izzy clenched her jaw. "Quit pestering that boy. He's not powerful enough to even draw a bear."

I bristled on Bolin's behalf, but the girl waved for her mother to come look at something. Had Bolin managed to slip away with Jasmine? He'd looked harried and probably would have slipped away with *anyone*, especially if it meant avoiding being outed as a quirky person with paranormal abilities in front of a roomful of people he might have to interact with in the coming years.

Izzy didn't want to leave me, but when her daughter held up something magical—hah, was that one of the bath bombs?—she frowned in concern and stalked away from me. Maybe the kid would accidentally drop it at her feet and entangle her. Were such actions frowned upon at upscale shindigs?

I took the opportunity to step into the room-like closet with Ivan.

"I've recently had something stolen." Ivan pointed toward the safe, the warped door now open. An air purifier hummed in the corner of the closet. The torching of the side of the safe had probably left an odor, though I didn't notice anything now. "And a lot of things *not* stolen." He gave me a significant look.

"How do you think I can help you?" I crouched to peer into the safe where envelopes, presumably full of cash, leaned against one side next to what looked like a fancy USB drive but was probably a crypto wallet. Tubes of coins—gold or silver?—also lay untouched.

"It was a peculiar thief." Ivan looked at me, as if to imply I was also peculiar, so it would be right up my alley.

Since I'd hoped to gather information on this very burglary, I wouldn't complain.

"And a peculiar item," he added. "A bracelet that grants—that's *supposed* to grant—the wearer the power of a werewolf for a time."

"Do you get such a thing at the same place where you buy your gold and bitcoin?"

"Of course not. All such artifacts were crafted centuries ago. You have to go to a dealer or buy them on the black market. Or go on a quest to hunt one down that was lost in a shipwreck or some such." He sounded wistful, as if he'd always wanted to do the latter.

Something told me this guy wasn't much like Duncan though. "I'm guessing you got it from a dealer."

He smirked wryly. "It was one of the first things I bought when I started making decent money."

I wagered *decent money* was seven figures a year.

"I was always a little envious of..." Ivan glanced toward the door, his sister's voice floating in to us. She was lecturing her daughter on accepting weird gifts from strangers. "Well, I suppose you can tell, and I needn't be coy with you."

"No." I hadn't missed his earlier correction about the artifact and suspected he'd used it from time to time. "No need for coyness here."

"The bracelet doesn't have the power to let a person change into a wolf—a bummer since that would be *amazing*—but it makes you strong and agile and fast for a while. Or it's supposed to." He shrugged elusively.

"Are such traits useful to a real estate developer?"

"Sure, if you want to carry toilets around." Ivan winked. "I've had the bracelet for twenty years, and it's sentimental to me. Also helpful on the tennis court."

"Where it's useful to be strong and agile?"

"It is. Though I'd never put such a tool to use. That would be cheating. But because it's sentimental, I would pay to get it back."

"I... might come across it. I've been dealing with artifact thieves of my own." I wished I'd taken photos of Radomir and Abrams, if only to see if this guy had ever chanced across them. "It's possible they're the same thieves that robbed you. They're collecting artifacts related to werewolves for reasons I haven't yet figured out."

"Strength and agility."

I doubted Radomir or Abrams played a lot of tennis but said, "Could be," with a shrug. "I don't suppose you got any footage of the thieves? Or hair or other, er, bodily essences that they left behind? The person I mentioned who is good at helping me find people can use such things."

"Oh, a forensics scientist with a microscope?"

"An alchemist with a cat familiar." I decided that since he knew about werewolves, he would believe that other paranormal beings existed.

Ivan blinked. "Does the cat play an integral role?"

"I don't think so. I've actually not seen it yet. Apparently, it hates my scent."

"Because..." He waved at me.

"I gather. I don't otherwise do anything to pester cats."

"You just exude the aura of a predator?"

"So I've been told." I cocked my head and regarded him. I'd believed him entirely normal, but if he could detect that...

"My sister said so. Maybe if I had my bracelet back, I could tell myself." Ivan looked wistfully at the safe, then must have remembered something because he snapped his fingers. "The police investigator found some hair on the safe that wasn't mine. They're supposedly analyzing it, but I haven't heard anything back. There was a chunk in that hinge there. One of the thieves may have caught his hair when he was bending low to destroy my safe."

I peered close and spotted a couple of lingering strands. "Do you have a baggie I could put this in?"

"Absolutely. And I'll grab the footage of the thieves too. It's from the parking lot and not very good, but maybe it'll help you." Ivan strode out of the closet.

I gripped my chin and stared at the safe, considering if there were any other questions I might ask that would help me with my various quests. I hadn't learned much that I hadn't already known. If I found the sword, maybe I would stumble across Ivan's bracelet at the same time, but it wasn't my priority.

"If you're thinking of stealing anything, you'd better reconsider," came a cool voice from the doorway.

Izzy had returned, sans her kid. She stood naked, her clothes tossed onto the bed. Her eyes had a feral glint, and I sensed her on the verge of changing.

"I'm not a thief." I stood straight, arms wide and innocent, though I doubted I could walk out without a fight.

"No? You're a murderer."

"It was a fight, not murder, and Raoul died in the heat of battle." I licked my lips, struggling to get words out to defend my actions that night. Since I'd never forgiven myself, how could I expect this stranger to forgive me?

"You killed him." Her voice was savage, almost a growl, and she dropped to all fours as the change came over her.

10

As Izzy changed, I tore off my own clothes, ribs twinging to remind me that I hadn't fully healed from the explosion. It didn't matter. I had no choice but to defend myself.

There would be repercussions from turning into a wolf and fighting another wolf in the bedroom of a wealthy real estate developer. That also didn't matter. Other concerns stampeded out the door when Izzy looked up at me, icy eyes savage, white-and-gray fur coating her sleek lupine body, her jaws open, her fangs dagger sharp.

My magic roared through me, my skin heating uncomfortably from within as my power dropped me to all fours, my torso and limbs shifting. By the time my foe charged into the closet at me, I'd finished changing, and I met her snapping jaws with rapid and powerful bites of my own.

As a wolf, I was larger and more muscular, but her fangs scored me, grazing my shoulder, as she fought with frenzy—with hatred. If I wasn't careful, she would kill me.

I struggled to feel indignation. In her eyes, this was retaliation from a family member over Raoul's death... If she killed me, would it even be wrong?

My instincts protected me, not allowing my conflicted feelings to get in the way of the fight. I leaped and dodged, avoiding her furious fangs and lunging in to bite whenever an opening appeared. I didn't want to kill her, only force her to leave me alone, but as my blood heated further, frustration making my attacks savage, I worried another member of the Cascade Crushers would end up dead at my feet.

Considering she'd been an elegant-looking woman, my enemy was a scrappy fighter. She fought more like an alley cat than a wolf, throwing in swipes with her paws as well as using her body like a wrestler. More than once, she crashed into me as she tried to force me back into shoe racks and hangers full of dangling trousers. We ended up on the carpeted floor of the closet, thrashing about, drawing blood and leaving spatters on the beige weave.

A door thumped open nearby. Someone had to have heard our fight. Maybe *everyone* had.

The realization that a stream of humans might rush in and see us—or be injured because they drew too close—gave me an incentive to end the battle. Using my greater strength and weight to my advantage, I shoulder-butted my foe, ramming her against the safe.

She yelped when she clipped it. I sprang atop her, bearing her to the floor. She snapped at me, but I knocked her maw aside with my own. Snarling, I lowered my fangs to her throat, half an inch from sinking them in.

Remembering that my human side didn't want this enemy dead, I paused. Further, I sensed someone looking into the closet, gaping at us and also the clothing, shoes, and broken shelves scattered everywhere. Our onlooker held a clear plastic bag with a couple of tiny hairs in it. Two gray-haired men in dark attire gaped in from behind his shoulders.

"Do you... need help, Izzy?" The closest man grabbed a sports racket off a shelf.

Such a mediocre weapon didn't worry me, but I lifted my jaws from my attacker's throat. I hadn't intended to kill her, regardless.

The icy expression that the female wolf gave me didn't suggest she would thank me later.

Snout up, I walked out of the closet, not so much as glancing at the racket. The man—Ivan, wasn't it?—stepped aside, letting me pass without taking a swing. The other two men backed all the way to the door of the room, one fumbling for the knob as they continued to gape at me.

Only as I sat on my haunches near the bed did I remember that my clothes remained inside the closet, buried somewhere under the mess. The other wolf growled and pushed herself to her feet. She looked at Ivan and growled again.

"Touchy, touchy," he muttered and closed the closet door on her.

So she could change back into a human in privacy? *Her* clothes were on the bed.

Ivan noticed them and skirted me to grab them. He opened the closet door to toss them inside. That prompted another growl, my enemy more irritated by the whole situation than thankful to anyone, I guessed.

"So..." Ivan shooed the other two men out of the bedroom— what rumors would they start about this?—and lowered the racket as he eyed me. "I can see why you would have an aptitude for security. You're, uhm, huge."

I rippled my lips to show him my fangs.

"Yeah, those are huge too. Did you attack my sister or the other way around?"

I lifted my snout again, turning my face toward a window. With the battle past, my magic was fading. Too bad I couldn't leave this great human hive and run to the woodlands to hunt before changing back.

"She started it, huh? She's been suspicious of you all night, but I know the Sylvans. They wouldn't hire someone with bad character. Kashvi, in particular, doesn't take crap from anyone. And I gather they—or at least Rory—know... about that." Ivan waved at my wolfness.

The magic faded, leaving me crouching naked near his bed. Why hadn't anyone grabbed *my* clothes?

"I'm less certain if he knows about *that*." Ivan's second wave indicated my nudity. His eyes crinkled with humor, though a thump from the closet made the expression fade. He knocked lightly on the door. "Are you okay, Izzy? Do you need a ride to the ER?"

The door opened, and Izzy stalked out, fully dressed again though her shoes were missing and her hair looked like it had been blow-dried by a tornado. She gave me a frosty look, her brother *almost* as frosty of one, and flung open the bedroom door to stalk out. The stalking faltered as numerous people who must have been listening with their ears close scattered. Without looking back, she strode away.

"You two have history, I gather." Ivan handed me the baggie.

"Apparently." I couldn't remember having encountered Izzy before, but she had to be seven or eight years younger than I, so she would have been a child when Raoul died and her pack left the area. "You're not, er, weren't affiliated with the Cascade Crushers?"

"My father was. He hooked up with my mother on a hiatus from the pack before going back and marrying one of his own kind. My single mom got to raise me on her own. I should have been bitter about that, I suppose, but I mostly wished my father would come back and do wolfish things with me. You know, take me hunting and fishing and camping."

"I think those are dad-ish things in general." Aware of my nudity, I padded into the closet to dig out my clothes. My ribs twinged as I bent, and blood trickled down my arm from a fresh puncture wound in my shoulder.

"Yeah. Do you need any help? Or can I take *you* to the ER?"

"I'm fine." A drop of my blood landed on the carpet. Even though we'd already stained it, I grimaced. "Sorry about that. Maybe I could use a Band-Aid."

"That bite mark is an inch deep."

"Two Band-Aids?"

Ivan snorted and stepped into the bathroom. I'd found my clothes and shoes by the time he returned with gauze, a roll of bandage, and a damp washcloth.

"Allow me. I always offer rides, but I'm aware of the werewolf aversion to treatment in normal medical facilities."

"We're not normal people."

"Oh, I'm aware of that too." Ivan winked and dabbed my wound.

I tried to decide if he was flirting with me and if I needed to mention that I was seeing someone else and wasn't available. He hadn't ogled me when I was naked, but that could mean that he had manners, not that he lacked interest.

Deciding it didn't matter one way or another at this time, I stood still while he pressed the gauze to my wound and wrapped the bandage under my armpit and around my shoulder.

"May I have your number?" he asked when he was done.

Oh, hell. He *was* interested.

"I'm seeing someone," I blurted.

"I meant so I can text you the photos from the parking lot." Ivan held up his phone, showing a grainy picture of two men getting onto motorcycles parked away from the influence of the streetlamps.

"Oh. Uhm, yes. Sorry."

We exchanged numbers, and Ivan texted the photos. I didn't look closely at them other than to note that one of the brutes was large and muscular enough to be one of Radomir's potion-swilling thugs. And the other... Had I seen him in the parking lot of Sylvan Serenity wielding a makeshift cudgel as he rode around on his motorcycle?

"I *would* be available for coffee sometime if you're interested." Ivan stepped back, leading me out of the closet. "Or hot steamy sex with no strings attached."

I opened my mouth but didn't know what to say.

"I'm jesting of course. Unless that strikes your fancy. In which case it's a genuine offer. I'm divorced and available for anything up to and equaling vacations to tropical locales and torrid late-night hotel trysts." His smirk suggested he didn't expect me to take him up on that.

"Fifteen minutes ago, you were suspicious of me, and I, uhm, beat up your sister."

"That's less of a deterrent than you might think. We've always had an edgy relationship. She was Dad's favorite, after all."

Ivan opened the bedroom door, not keeping me longer. The people who'd been drawn by the fight noises had scattered, but Jasmine and Bolin stood nearby and looked toward us.

"And as I said before," Ivan said quietly, "I'll offer a monetary reward if you're able to find those men and retrieve my bracelet. And if the Sylvans sell that property and you need a job, let me know. I'm *positive* I can find someone who can use a person with your skills."

"My property-management skills? Or my security skills?"
"*Both.*"

With the baggie of hair strands in my hand, I headed for the exit, hoping Jasmine wouldn't mind leaving early. I glimpsed Izzy, her wild locks now combed, though she still looked disheveled as she glared at me from the fireplace, the two older men who'd witnessed my change standing nearby. Izzy gripped a cocktail—definitely not a *mock*tail—like she wanted to throw it at me. One of the men was holding what looked like a scotch on the rocks and lifted it toward me in a salute.

I shook my head. Whether I'd seen the last of Izzy or not, I didn't know, but I'd had enough of this party.

Jasmine waved a goodbye to Bolin, then jogged to catch up with me. "That was amazing. I had no idea that you were a master at this stuff."

"What stuff?"

"*Networking.*" Jasmine glanced back. "OMG, Ivan MacGregor is checking out your ass. And he's not the only one."

I rubbed my face as a doorman appeared, opening the way to the hallway. "Is that the kind of networking you want to do?"

"Well, I'd prefer to get a job offer on merit and without having to put out, but you've got a bunch of rich old men who aren't going to forget your face—or any of your other attributes."

"That's what I'm afraid of."

11

As Jasmine drove me back to Sylvan Serenity, I spotted Duncan's Roadtrek by the pond behind the convenience store. Had more trouble found the place?

"Uh-oh. Let me out here, will you?" I didn't see any motorcycle thugs in the parking lot, just a few teenagers loitering around a car, probably waiting for an older friend to come out with alcohol. That didn't mean Duncan hadn't sussed out something about to go down.

"You're having an urge for a slushie?" Jasmine signaled to turn into the store's parking lot, but I pointed her toward the handful of spaces by the pond's small dock. "Oh, you're having an urge for a Duncan."

"To see what he's up to, anyway."

"It's a moonlit night. You two should go for a hunt."

"In Shoreline?"

"No, nobody should hunt in Shoreline." Jasmine pulled into the spot beside the van.

The pond wasn't lit at night, and there weren't any other cars present.

"I remember you catching a rabbit and eating it on my apartment's doorstep," I said.

"Only because I got bored waiting *hours* for you and needed a snack."

"You could have raided my fridge."

Duncan stood at the end of the dock with a couple of his magnets. He gazed back at us and lifted a hand in greeting.

It appeared to be a calm moonlit fishing session, nothing suggesting he expected trouble, but he'd already investigated this pond. Other than grime-coated car keys and a rusty shopping cart missing wheels, he hadn't discovered anything that would prompt a return visit, at least not that I'd witnessed.

"I'll keep that in mind for next time," Jasmine said. "Do you want me to wait?"

"That's okay." I slid out of her car. "I'll get a ride back with Duncan."

"Or you two could stay here and check out the bed in his van. The stars and moon are out, and there's a pond and romantic ambiance."

One of the teenagers in front of the store belched, then laughed loudly.

"Romantic," I said.

"Well, maybe you could drive somewhere else."

"Good idea. Thanks for the ride tonight."

"No problem. Sorry we didn't learn anything more useful. Or get job offers. Though I think that MacGregor would hire you. He was into your female attributes."

"I'd rather be hired because I do a good job in a professional capacity than because of my ass." Or because I could turn into a wolf in someone's bedroom closet.

"The world doesn't work that way, Aunt Luna."

"You're being cynical for a twenty-something. Maybe *you* should go for a hunt."

Jasmine looked out the window toward the moon. "That does sound appealing. Either that or sitting in my parents' hot tub."

"Are you *sure* you want to get your own place? You've got a lot of nice amenities there."

"True, but I'm ready to be independent. Besides, condos have hot tubs too."

"Even barebones condos overlooking the freeway?"

Jasmine made a face. "I might be lucky to even get a *bathtub* there."

I waved again, then walked toward the dock, the chilly breeze making me pull my jacket close. January wasn't the most appealing time of year for romantic moonlit interludes.

"Are you rescuing more fish from coin toxicity?" I asked when I reached Duncan.

"No. If there are coins down there, they're too deep for me to pluck out by hand, and, as I mentioned to you before, your American currency isn't magnetic." Duncan held up one of his fishing implements, a long rusty nail attached to it, to demonstrate what his tools usually attracted.

"You could get out your SCUBA gear."

"If you drink another of those unappealing potions, and I deem it necessary to buy beverages for you, I'll consider it."

"Are you short on funds? You've been here quite a while without..." I turned my palm upward and decided not to say *doing any productive work*. After all, he'd found my pack's missing medallion. That was plenty productive. But I hadn't seen him do anything that people paid for. Few of the rusty objects that he'd extracted in my presence had any value, even at a pawn shop with low standards.

"Working?" Duncan smirked, probably reading my thoughts.

"Being paid."

"You've paid me numerous times."

"If you're talking about the gas money I've tucked under the bobblehead doll on your dash, that's not a living wage."

He hadn't spent any of it anyway. He'd spoken of saving it all to buy me a gift.

Duncan waved airily and plopped his magnet into the water again. "My funds are fine. I enjoy the hunt for treasure. I'll admit I don't usually raid koi ponds for my finds, but..."

"You've been sticking close to me." I suspected he'd resorted to investigating such anemic bodies of water because he hadn't wanted to be far away if trouble found me.

"You're in danger often." His voice was grave. "I trust nothing untoward happened at your networking event? I did consider sneaking into the party in case enemies found you."

"Nothing too major happened, no. Unless you count an Arizonian werewolf from my past coming out of the woodwork to attack me in a billionaire's bedroom closet."

Duncan blinked.

"He might only be a multimillionaire," I said. "We didn't get into his financials."

"Are you okay?"

"Yeah, but I don't think I'll be invited down to visit his sister in Arizona anytime soon." I decided not to bring up Raoul.

"Hm." Duncan slowly dragged his magnet alongside the dock. "There aren't many excellent bodies of water to investigate down there."

"There aren't many bodies of water of any kind. I've also heard you get cactus thorns in your paw pads."

"Quite."

"When I'm forced to get a new job, I will ideally keep the employment hunt to the Pacific Northwest." Technically, since my kids were grown and gone, I didn't *need* to remain here, but my stomach knotted at the idea of leaving the area. Even though I hadn't, these past couple of months, kept up with friends I'd made during my years of attempting to be normal, I'd started reestablishing relations with members of the pack, and getting to know Jasmine had been fun. "I don't want to leave, damn it," I whispered.

The words were more for me than Duncan, but he paused at dragging his rope and raised his eyebrows. Enough moonlight shone upon his face to see the sympathy and concern there. That touched me, soothing some of my anxiety. It was good to have met someone who understood what I was and cared anyway.

"I'm grousing again about the apartment complex being for sale," I explained. "I know I need to be proactive and look for work and a new home, something affordable, but it's hard."

"You *have* been busy with other matters. And it's your most foul nemeses who are attempting to buy your home, so you're understandably distracted by trying to figure out what nefarious acts they're plotting."

"Tell me about it. But when their deal falls through, as I'm sure it will, someone else will put in an offer. Despite a few snide comments about the place at that networking event, there's been interest."

"It's well-maintained, and the parking-lot unit has a lovely view of the woods."

"There's no parking-lot unit."

Duncan smiled.

"Unless you mean your van."

"I'm surprised you haven't attempted to charge me rent for that spot yet. Were I situated for so long in one of this country's RV campgrounds, I would expect weekly charges."

"I *did* notice that you attached your hose to one of our spigots yesterday morning. I should send you a water bill."

"I should think so." His smile faded as he gazed at the pond, the silvery moonlight reflecting on the surface, shimmering with the movements of his rope.

"What brought you over here tonight?"

I'd obliquely asked that already but not directly. Of course, he could avoid answering questions, either way. And, as the silence stretched, I assumed he would do exactly that.

After a few minutes, Duncan took a slow breath. "I've had a few... twinges."

"Twinges? Like from the injuries we got when that house blew up?" I touched my bandaged ribs.

"I've mostly healed from those, but I've been getting some headaches—stabbing pains, you might call them. Back behind here." Duncan touched the scar on his forehead.

My earlier anxiety returned, a heavy pit in my stomach.

"And I've felt less hale than usual. I woke up nauseated and threw up this morning."

"I don't suppose it was just a hangover?"

"I haven't been drinking the questionable concoctions at El Gato Mágico."

"Have you been back there?" I didn't care about the paranormal bar, but I was afraid to ask for more details about his illness.

"A couple of times. After Francisco got less skittish around me, he learned to mix up one of my favorite drinks. But I wasn't there last night. I haven't been there this week at all." Duncan shrugged. "Maybe it's nothing. A wee bug." He pinched two fingers together, almost touching the tips. "But I don't get sick often."

"Werewolves have hardy constitutions."

"Quite." Duncan lowered his hand and repeated, "Maybe it's nothing."

I gripped the cool, splintered railing of the dock, certain that it wasn't *nothing*.

"Or maybe it's what Abrams suggested?" I whispered.

Duncan shrugged. "He's told me that tale before, that I am— *was* linked to that device. Supposedly, he made the magical connection in my youth, earlier than I can remember. Abrams wanted to ensure my good behavior, to make sure I wouldn't steal or destroy the control device and run away. I never knew if he was telling the truth or not, and when I escaped... Well, I got away, so I assumed he'd been lying. Of course, I believed at the time that he'd died in the burning of his castle. Even though he didn't, he must have been injured, too injured to call me back with the device until I was out of its influence. So, you see, I never got a chance to find out if its destruction would affect me the way he promised."

"Until now. I'm sorry, Duncan. I didn't mean— Like I said, my plan was originally to *take* it, not destroy it."

He waved away my words. "I don't blame you for anything."

Maybe not, but I blamed myself.

"They made enemies of you, threatening you and your family. It made sense for you to strike at them—and to deny them a powerful magically manipulated ally." Face rueful, his wave shifted to encompass himself. "I'm only now accepting that maybe it's not all bollocks, that Abrams was right, and I could, as they say in this country, end up pushing up daisies."

I thought about sharing that nobody said that anymore—he'd probably read the phrase in a book. But it didn't matter. All that mattered was that he might die. Not nobly in battle or on a hunt but to a magical curse.

"Do you think handing over the artifacts that they want could be a solution to your problem?" I asked, thinking of the special-delivery letter he'd received.

"Oh, moon shadows, no. They're trying to take advantage of the situation and manipulate us. I can't see how anyone but a powerful crafter, the kind the world no longer knows, could alter existing artifacts and use their magic to some ends other than which they were made for." Duncan squinted at me. "Don't you consider giving the case or anything else to them."

"I do love it when men give me orders," I said, though my heart wasn't in the snark.

"I'd say it was a strong suggestion, but that's not true. I must absolutely forbid you from making that sacrifice. The medallions belong to your pack, and they may even be able to protect them and our kind in general more than we've yet discovered. This definitely has the power to protect its wearer." Duncan touched the medallion on his chest. "Maybe not from fire, but it overrode the manipulative magic of the other control device, and I don't doubt that it can do more. And that case and the artifact within? I felt firsthand its power."

"Yeah."

Too bad it hadn't been enough to heal my mother of her cancer.

"For all we know," Duncan continued, "the continuing existence of werewolves is tied to those artifacts and others like them. To the medallions certainly. There's little magic left within the earth, and we need magic to exist. To live." He fell silent, his gaze toward the pond again.

Since I didn't know what to say, I leaned against him, my shoulder to his. He pulled up his magnet, rested it on the railing, and wrapped an arm around me.

"Do you want more kids, Luna?"

I blinked at the abrupt topic shift and surprised myself with the answer that came to mind. It wasn't a firm *no*. Instead, I said, "I... didn't think I did."

"Did something change?"

"Now that I'm a werewolf again, well... I don't know. It's not something that would have crossed my mind if my mother hadn't kept bringing it up—and I hate that she wants to pressure me and *you* about that—but a part of me wonders what it would be like to have werewolf pups." *Your* pups, I thought but didn't say. The last thing I wished was for Duncan to believe I was like my mother in any way, or wanted anything from him. Besides, we hadn't even had sex yet. It was silly to wonder what children with him would be like. "When I was raising my sons, I *did* often wish for a little girl."

"In addition to them?"

"Or instead of," I said dryly. "Boys are a lot of work."

"And girls are easy?"

"They don't usually put their fists through the drywall and go through phases where they're disassembling all the electronics in the house. I went through *four* toasters when Austin was in middle school. And I had to repair the drywall and paint numerous times due to testosterone-driven temper tantrums."

"Something tells me that girls may come with challenges too." Duncan gazed at me through his eyelashes.

"Funny that you'd look at me while you say that."

"Isn't it?" He smiled again, but it was fleeting. "The reason I asked... Well, I was curious. Over the years, I've wondered from time to time about what having children might be like, but I always dismissed the idea. I love travel so much that I could never imagine being tied down in one place. But now that I've been presented with this... *this*.." He tapped his scar. "Well, it's forced me to realize I could die without leaving any offspring to carry on my blood."

"Your scientist-crafted laboratory blood is weird."

"True, but, surely, someone would want it? Your mother thinks it has appeal."

"She just wants grandkids with the power to kick a lot of ass. It's a typical thing for a werewolf mother to desire."

"Since I never had a mother, I'll have to take your word for that." Duncan held my gaze for a moment before looking toward the water again. The moon had gone behind a tree, leaving the silver beam on the surface broken in two. "This turn of events has had me rethinking things a touch. Maybe... having a few regrets."

"You'll have to find a way not to die, at least not yet. Then there's still time for you to have kids."

"Hm."

I didn't know if that noise meant he didn't believe he could beat this curse or if he hadn't yet decided that he wanted kids. It sounded like he was mostly at the musing—and regrets—phase.

"You can have children and travel, you know," I pointed out. "Either their mother could stay at home with them, or the whole family could be nomadic and have adventures. Then you'd have the opportunity to teach them to ride a bike—or fish rusty bikes out of a lake."

"Oh goodness, that sounds wonderful."

If not for the grim undercurrent, I would have laughed. Only he could say something like that and be serious.

"I hadn't thought of taking children *on* my travels." Duncan gazed at me and touched a finger to my jaw. "You're a delightful woman, Luna Valens."

"I am," I said, though I hoped he wasn't envisioning *me* cavorting around the world with him, a pack of our offspring in tow. I didn't even want to leave my apartment in Shoreline. Not to be nomadic, anyway. A vacation adventure here and there might be okay.

Musings that wouldn't matter unless Duncan lived and we had a relationship. His eyebrow twitched, not in some sardonic facial expression, but because, if the accompanying wince was an indicator, he had a headache. Or stabs of pain in his skull.

On the verge of tears, I opened my mouth to reiterate the need to find a solution to his problem, but he took my parted lips as an invitation and smoothed his face and kissed me.

It was a tender kiss rather than one filled with fiery passion. It held the longing and regret he'd voiced, the uncertainty about whether he would be able to pursue the future we'd spoken about. I tried to comfort him, returning the kiss in kind, but I also couldn't help but wonder if we should make the most of the time we had.

Not here though. One of the teenagers in the parking lot whistled, and his friends laughed. My phone rang. The romance of a moonlit night would have to wait. Clouds were wafting in anyway, the air smelling like rain might come the next day.

Duncan sighed and leaned back.

I frowned in confusion at the name on my phone. It was Minato, the owner of the convenience store next to the pond. Was it possible the teenagers had committed a crime that he hoped I could handle?

"Hello?"

"Ms. Valens. Thank you for taking my call this late at night."

"Uh, no problem." I glanced at the clock on my phone. It was creeping up on ten p.m., but my tenants often called that late to report water leaks and other time-sensitive problems. Occasionally problems that *weren't* time sensitive too. "What's up?"

Perhaps having similar thoughts as I'd had, Duncan gazed up at the teenagers. Other than the underaged drinking, they didn't seem to be partaking in any crimes. One even pointed at me and gave Duncan a thumbs-up.

"It is a quiet night at my store, perhaps because you are standing guard nearby—"

Standing guard. Right.

"—but a business acquaintance of mine called and wishes to know if you are available to stop a crime. He is one of the ones I've spoken with about putting together funds to pay you for protecting the small businesses in the neighborhood."

I kept telling him they didn't need to pay me to help out, but since I'd done nothing to solve the problem, I didn't bring that up again. "I... guess I'm available."

Duncan sighed wistfully—maybe he'd also been thinking of

activities we might want to engage in if time was running out. But he didn't object.

"My acquaintance is Harold Chen. He owns the discount movie theater a few blocks away. Some of the local gang members rode their motorcycles into his parking lot, strode inside without paying, helped themselves to concessions, and are now watching a movie. The police said they would send a patrol car over when they have time, but they categorized the crime as minor and sounded busy with more pressing matters. Unfortunate, because these small crimes pave the way for larger ones. Further, one movie-goer reported that one of the men grew lewd with her and tried to grab her. When my acquaintance confronted him, the man punched him and said to make it a private showing if he had a problem with complaints."

"We need to figure out who's in charge of those guys and put an end to their *gang*." I doubted Radomir and Abrams had anything to do with that. They were merely taking advantage of the locals being available to pester me.

"*Yes*," Minato said in agreement. "I will tell him you are coming."

"Maybe the one masterminding the thefts will be there." I shrugged apologetically at Duncan for needing to leave when he was feeling low.

"I'll go with you to check. We can continue our impromptu date."

"Jasmine did suggest we might want to go on a hunt together. That it would be romantic." I doubted she'd meant the hunt should be in a movie theater.

"I'm sure it will be."

12

WHEN WE DROVE UP TO THE THEATER, THE OWNER—HAROLD—WAS pacing outside the small box office. Since the last showing for the night had already started, there weren't many people around. Harold pushed a hand through his short graying hair and frowned uncertainly at Duncan's camper van until we parked and stepped out. Then his dark eyes widened with recognition, and he sprang upon me in relief.

I'd never seen him before but sensed, as with Minato's wife, a hint of power within him. Another member of the paranormal community as well as the business community. Funny how many magically-inclined people ended up working for themselves. Or maybe it wasn't. We tended to be quirky with attributes that didn't lend themselves well to normal employment.

"Ms. Valens." Harold pulled out his phone, tapping the photos app. "Thank you for coming. I can sense the lupine power rippling about you. It's *wonderful*."

"It has its moments."

When Duncan stepped up beside me, Harold looked at him,

lips parting in surprise. "You *also* have lupine power. It blazes like the sun."

"Nice of you to notice." Duncan bowed amiably toward him.

"Mine only ripples," I said.

"But the ripples are so lovely and appealing," Duncan said.

"Should that bolster me so that I don't feel lesser next to you?"

Duncan nodded, but Harold spoke again before he could reply.

"You are *both* magnificent. I know you will be able to handle this problem. These brutes are in the first theater inside." Harold showed us a photo he'd taken of the men raiding his concessions stand, helping themselves to popcorn and arms full of boxes of candy. Judging by how much they were taking, the police categorizing the crime as minor didn't seem right. That had to be hundreds of dollars' worth of snacks.

"Eating food like that, it's surprising they've amassed such bulk," Duncan murmured, flexing a biceps.

"Carbs are great for making you big," I said. "It's what they give cows before slaughter."

"Skittles and Junior Mints?"

"Well, corn and barley. I'm sure a cow would eat a Junior Mint if offered one."

Duncan shook his head and said, "Herbivores," in the same kind of superior way my mother might have. Leave it to werewolves to be snobby about other animals' dietary preferences.

Harold showed us another photo, the backs of the heads of the men who were sitting in the theater. One was looking toward him and giving the middle finger.

My breath caught. That was one of the faces from Ivan's security footage. It might be the guy who'd taken my sword, whose hair sample was, at that very second, in a baggie in my pocket.

I looked around the parking lot, as if the sword might be in the back seat of a car the thugs had driven over. Wishful thinking. Besides, they'd come on motorcycles. Several were parked on the cement walkway in front of the theater instead of in legal spots.

"If I had a knife, I would slash their tires to make sure they couldn't escape." Or if I'd had a *sword*. I missed that weapon more than I'd expected to, maybe because I was a quarter of the way to competent with a blade, now that I'd had lessons.

"I'll be happy to take care of that if you ensure there won't be repercussions to my establishment or myself," Harold said.

"Do it," I said. "And blame it on us. We're about to kick them out."

I nodded to Duncan, and he smiled agreeably.

Harold looked at me with such appreciation that he had to be seconds away from kissing me. He gave Duncan a similar look.

Duncan must have interpreted it the same way because he backed up, lifted a hand, and pointed at the front door. "They're that way, you say?"

"First door." Harold gestured toward it without kissing either of us.

Duncan and I headed for the entrance.

"Since I didn't bring any weapons, we're going to have to get furry," I told him, hoping I could call upon my magic for the second time that evening.

"I expected that." Duncan removed his jacket as we stepped inside, startling a pimple-faced teenager running a vacuum over the carpet.

The kid was sticking to a corner far from the theater door; he'd probably also had an unpleasant run-in with the thugs.

"I'd better take off my clothes before changing so I don't lose them, but I also feel we should talk to these guys and give them a chance to leave peacefully before we start biting them." My outfit had already dodged a bullet that night, and I was determined to keep it. Besides, the clothes cost more than a lot of the other garments in my wardrobe. I could wear them to the real estate meetup at the bowling alley.

"Perhaps you'd like to step into the loo and change, while I deliver an ultimatum to them?" Duncan suggested.

"You don't care about your clothes surviving a shift?"

"I'm quite fast at shucking them. I'm even wearing trousers with an elastic waistband tonight." Duncan slid a thumb into them and stretched them sideways to demonstrate.

"Sexy."

"The man makes the clothes, isn't that the saying?"

"Not quite."

Since the lobby was empty, with the owner busy out front, applying box cutters to tires, and the vacuum-wielder navigating down a hallway, I removed my shoes, socks, jacket, and phone without going into the bathroom. I loosened a few other items, Duncan doing the same beside me.

"I'll talk to them," I said. "I'm the supposed crime fighter for Shoreline now."

I didn't care about getting credit for stopping criminals, but Duncan would likely move on one day—because he adored travel, I told myself, *not* because he would die within weeks. I had to establish myself as the person the criminal element feared to cross. They needed to know that I could and would protect the neighborhood.

"Not supposed," Duncan said. "You undeniably fight crime. And you do it with wondrous aplomb."

"You didn't see me knee the brute in the backyard in the balls."

"Ball-kneeing can be done with aplomb. It's unfortunate that the house exploding kept me from witnessing your battle. I do enjoy watching you fight." His words were light and playful, but he gazed at me with pleasure, as if he truly did enjoy that.

My cheeks warmed at his appreciation, and I kissed him on

the cheek. "I like watching you fight too. And having you at my side."

"A most enjoyable place to be, my lady." He bowed to me, then strode forward and thrust open the door to the theater.

The sound of movie dialogue flowed out, a tense drama scene playing on the large screen. No heads turned in our direction, though I spotted the pack of thugs in prime center seats near the front. The rest of the movie-goers must have left along with the harassed woman that Harold had mentioned. It was a private showing.

Shouts on the screen made me wish I'd thought to ask the owner to turn off the movie. It would be hard to deliver an ultimatum over the noise.

Duncan let me head down the aisle toward the men, lingering to remove the rest of his clothing. He had to assume the thugs would reject my offer to leave peaceably. After all I'd endured from them, I didn't even want to make the offer, but the comic books I'd read to my sons in their youth ensured that was proper superhero etiquette.

"I heard you thugs didn't pay for that popcorn," I said loudly when the movie quieted.

As they turned around—yes, the thief from the security-camera footage was with them—the screen went dark. Harold had been emboldened by our arrival.

"Look who's butting into our lives again," one thug said.

"You've been butting into my life for weeks, asshole. Where's my sword?" I glared at the one from the camera. "And the wolf bracelet you helped steal?"

"Don't know what you're talking about, bitch. You get out or..." He trailed off, his gaze dropping to my side.

Duncan padded up on all fours, the hackles of his salt-and-pepper fur up. He growled at the men.

"*You* get out. Or don't, but know that I've decided to help clean up this town." I winced at the cheesy Western-movie delivery, but oh well.

One man reached into his jacket. My instincts warned me that more than one thug was armed, and did I detect a hint of magic? Silver bullets in a gun?

"If you dumbasses don't leave Shoreline," I said, "I'll make sure you're buried here. You can't stay unless you shape up and become good citizens. Instead of bullying others out of what they've worked hard for, you can leave offerings for the charities in town. Money, or good coffee or dark chocolate."

That was what charities needed, wasn't it?

With my own magic flowing through my veins and the change approaching, it was possible my words weren't that logical. I didn't care. I welcomed the power heating my blood for I had no doubt that this would turn into a battle.

"You bring the hand thing?" one man whispered to another as several stood.

"It's in my saddlebag. Just pound them the old-fashioned way."

"That hasn't worked yet." The first speaker glanced toward an exit door.

The man who'd been reaching into his jacket pulled out a handgun. He aimed it toward my head, but I was already dropping to all fours.

Duncan surged over the seats, springing at the gunman. I tried to tear off the rest of my clothing before the wolf took over, but I didn't manage to get everything. It was just as well. There wasn't time.

As the shooter fired, Duncan leaping into his chest and bearing him down between the seats, another guy ran into the aisle toward me. He tried to kick me, but I'd finished changing, and the instincts of the wolf took over.

I caught his leg with my jaws, biting down. At the same time, I yanked backward, pulling him off his feet. One of his pack mates jumped out, trying to knock me away from the fallen human. I bit him too, fangs sinking through his leather jacket and into his side.

Snarls and cries of pain came from my ally's fight. Another gunshot fired, but Duncan had knocked the weapon aside so the bullet went wide. He clamped down on the gun—and the owner's hand. Bone crunched, and metal crumpled. The man screamed. My ally let him go but only so he could spin to deal with another enemy.

Rapid thuds of boots on concrete sounded as one of the men ran toward the exit door.

Still battling the two foes in the aisle with me, I was tempted to let that one go, but he glanced back, and I glimpsed his face. It was familiar, more so than those of the others, and held significance to my human self. I couldn't remember why, but I trusted my feelings and leaped over a row of seats. I rushed toward the side door, determined to keep that man from escaping.

When I entered the aisle ahead of him, he spotted me and flailed his arms to halt himself. After he caught his balance, he slid a hand into his jacket. To pull out a firearm?

I leaped, aware of the danger, and smashed into his chest at the same time as he drew out the weapon. He pitched backward, his knuckles cracking against the wall. The firearm flew free. I stood on his chest, fangs inches from his face, and snarled to let him know I could end his life. But I had to convey something else to him, didn't I? What was it the human part of me desired?

"Radomir has it," the man blurted, wincing when a drop of my saliva landed on his cheek.

He jerked his arms up and tried to push me off, but I sank all of my weight onto him.

"He paid me for it. It's up north."

I snarled.

"Near Maple Falls," he blurted. "They've got a place up there.

Some kind of laboratory. It's where they're keeping all the stuff they pay to have stolen. I don't—"

A thud sounded near the front of the theater, followed by a lupine yelp of pain.

My head snapped up. My ally?

"Get that one," someone ordered. "She's weaker without him."

Magic surged from the center aisle, and Duncan cried out again. They had something capable of hurting him.

Fury swept through me, my tail going straight out as the wildness of the moon magic filled me, savagery replacing rational thoughts.

Thinking me distracted, the man on the floor twisted and reached for his gun. Furious because these people were hurting Duncan, I lashed out with my fangs. Guided by the moon's raw power, I bit over and over, taking out my frustrations on the man.

When he moved no more, I ran to the front of the theater, to where I'd heard my ally's cry.

His back was to the screen, and two unmoving bodies lay before him, but he was also injured and did not put weight on one of his forelimbs. A single man still stood in the aisle, aiming a gun at him but also pointing a fist with a glowing ruby ring on it.

Duncan shook his head, as if fighting off magic attacking him. Or... what if it was an illness? I could smell that something tainted him, something unfamiliar and dangerous.

Determined to protect my ally, I ran around the front row of seats. The man flinched when he saw me coming and whipped both ring and gun in my direction. His finger twitched on the trigger, and I lowered my body, but I kept running. A bullet whizzed over my head, doing no harm, but a ripple of electricity flowed from the ring and caught me, biting into my skin like a thousand mosquitoes.

Snarling, I crashed into the man, more momentum than focused attack. The intense irritation to my skin as well as my worry for Duncan made me snap my jaws without hesitation. A dozen times, they sank into flesh before the man pitched to the ground, rolling onto his side and flinging his arms over his head. He tried to crawl away, and the attack from the ring stopped, but I didn't want to let him go. He'd hurt Duncan, and he was a plague to this human settlement.

I would have finished him off, the same as the other, but a cheer from the back of the theater made me lift my head. Was this a new threat?

A slender graying man held up an electronic device, pointing a tiny lens toward me.

"Amazing!" he cried.

Wary, I rippled my lips and growled at him.

"Oh," he blurted. "I'll wait outside."

The owner of this place, I decided, thoughts trickling back into my mind and my blood cooling slightly. He'd requested that we come.

The injured man was crawling up the aisle on his knees and elbows, dragging himself away from me. I could yet finish him off, but a moan came from behind me. My ally.

He'd turned back into a human, the wolf magic leaving him early. Or maybe he'd chosen to have it leave since our enemies were either dead or escaping, too injured to continue to be a threat? He lay on his side, gripping his head, and moaned again.

I padded forward, my hackles lowering, and nosed him with concern. A bullet had grazed his shoulder, and the scent of his blood hung in the air, mingling with the smells of similar odors from the fallen men. But my ally's blood was distinct, the power of the Old World in it. There was also that taint I'd smelled earlier. Some vile magic that afflicted him.

"Sorry, Luna," he whispered, still gripping his head. "That was a pathetic showing." Grimacing, he pushed himself into a sitting position. "I didn't want to admit it before. Thought it was just a headache that came and went, and that I was a little off, but I also lacked my usual strength in that battle."

I looked over the fallen and those too injured to crawl away. He'd defeated as many enemies as I, but he did appear diminished. Ill. Or... cursed?

A human memory floated into my wolf mind, something he'd shared with me earlier. He was dying.

13

BACK IN HUMAN FORM AND DRESSED IN MOST OF MY CLOTHES, I walked out of the theater with Duncan. The mock turtleneck had disappeared, but my jacket hid that. Duncan had also found his clothes and dressed, though the bullet wound in his shoulder was bleeding through his shirt. He looked beleaguered, with uncharacteristic bags under his eyes and his hair more tousled than usual.

My stomach knotted with worry.

"I didn't realize it would affect my ability to fight." Duncan huffed out a breath and gazed skyward, toward the clouds that had wafted in and obscured the moon and stars. "I didn't even fully realize... didn't *want* to... Sorry, Luna," he said again. "I hope I didn't leave you in a bind."

"You didn't. You still kicked plenty of ass." I didn't want him to think I believed him any lesser because he was losing some of his strength. "And don't apologize. This is all my fault."

I shook my head glumly as we approached the thugs' motorcycles. Harold had done as he'd promised, slashing the tires, so even those men who'd escaped the theater hadn't been able to ride off.

They'd departed on foot, leaving trails of blood. Some hadn't departed at all. I grimaced at the memory of losing my rational mind, of giving in to the wild savagery of the werewolf magic and killing.

A part of me believed the criminals deserved that fate, but the law wouldn't agree. And at least one of those police officers knew now what I was, knew that if a wolf was responsible for deaths in Shoreline, *I* would be the one to question. Worse, Harold had recorded some of the fight. Even though I'd been the wolf, I remembered him holding his phone up. Since we'd helped him, I *hoped* he wouldn't turn the footage over to the police, but even if all he did was put it on a social-media site, it might lead the authorities back to me.

"What a night." I sighed. "It wasn't as romantic as I'd hoped."

"Maybe we should have gone on an actual hunt." Duncan poked into the various bags attached to the abandoned motorcycles. "There's something magical in here. Didn't that guy say—"

"It's not the sword." My time as a wolf was always a blur when I returned to human form, but I did recall the man I'd pinned spitting out that information. Hadn't he said Radomir's name? And that it was in... a laboratory near Maple Falls? That was it.

I scowled at the memory of Radomir capturing Austin up there and my battle in the vacation cabin on the lake. At least my son was now safely across the country, finishing his Air Force training.

"No, but I think..." Duncan drew out a hand device with ring attachments and a purple oval gem in the center.

The last time I'd seen it had been in the parking lot of Sylvan Serenity, and that gem had been glowing and attacking my brain. I bared my teeth at it.

"This and that magical ring the man inside was wearing..." Duncan tipped his thumb over his shoulder toward the theater. "They're unlikely items for thugs off the street to have."

"Bribes from Radomir. More valuable than mere money."

"Indeed."

We'd already suspected that Radomir had started working with these guys, so we hadn't learned anything new other than receiving a lead to the sword's location.

"Did you spend time at a laboratory in Maple Falls?" I asked. "When you were under Radomir's control? Oh, you said he rented that cabin, right?"

The little A-frame on the lake wouldn't have counted as a *laboratory* though. Inside and out, it had looked like a normal vacation home.

"Yes, but, most recently, when he called me to give me orders, he drew me to a hotel up there, and he was in the middle of packing. He didn't mention where he was going next. I don't think he ever believed he had me fully under control. He probably suspected I would happily tell you everything I learned about him whenever I got the chance. Which was correct." Duncan smiled faintly. "You're my confidante, you know."

"I thought I was only your chocolate supplier."

"That's *why* you're my confidante." He rested a hand over his heart, then handed the artifact to me. What I would do with it, I didn't know.

I checked the rest of the bags on the motorcycles, hoping I would find Ivan's bracelet in there, but it was a vain hope since my senses didn't pick up on anything else magical. Too bad. If I could have found everything without needing Rue to make another Elixir of Locus to inflict on my tortured esophagus, that would have been ideal.

"I'm going to ask her about you," I decided.

Duncan, not able to read my thoughts, asked, "What?"

"Maybe Rue has some ideas about how to fix you."

"Fix? What few flaws I have add whimsy and character."

"You *know* what I mean. You can't *die.*" Frustrated, I almost hurled the hand artifact into the parking lot, but I held back. It might provide a clue.

"I would prefer to avoid that fate, yes. I'll cheerfully visit the alchemist with you, but I'm skeptical of her ability to heal me of this curse." Duncan waved toward the scar on his forehead.

"We have to start somewhere. We might not have much time."

"I am aware of that. Finding and questioning Abrams is on my mind. Since he *placed* the curse, he likely has more expertise on the matter than anyone else."

"True. Do you have any idea about where to find him?"

"Not yet, but I will." Duncan nodded firmly.

The determination in his eyes relieved me. I'd worried he believed his fate inevitable and wouldn't fight it. But he gazed toward the north with speculation. I hoped he was scheming at that very moment about how to find Abrams—and wring the information out of him with his clawed bipedfuris fingers.

I walked the hand artifact over to a light and took a couple of photos of it, then texted them to Jasmine.

If your dad is pining for more research opportunities, I would be curious to know if he can dig up anything on this.

Since it was probably a random doodad that Abrams or Radomir had picked up years ago, I doubted it could lead us to them, but one never knew.

I'll show him, came her prompt reply. *The license plate didn't pan out. It's linked to the address of the lavender farm that's up for sale.*

I suppose that isn't surprising.

I'll get Dad on this though.

Thanks. I showed Duncan my phone when he looked over. "Shall we visit Rue while we're waiting on our researcher? The good news is that if she *can* heal you, it'll likely be in the form of a sumptuous potion that will perk your tastebuds right up."

"Your tastebuds looked more tortured than perked when you drank her last potion."

"They were perkily tortured."

"My lady, I believe you're lying to me."

"I didn't want to squelch your optimism for an alchemical solution."

"I'll accept *any* solution that we can find. If I must imbibe a potion, will you buy me chocolate-flavored espresso drinks to wash down the taste?"

"Of course. I'll even fish coins out of the koi pond if I need the funds."

"Dear Luna, I believe you're falling in love with me."

"It's your charm. It's polishing my jaded edges." I leaned against him and blinked a few times, trying to stave off the tears forming in my eyes.

"It does have that effect on ladies." Duncan wrapped his arms around me, and we stood there until rain started falling, dampening the rest of my face.

14

RUE DIDN'T HAVE ANY IMMEDIATE KNOWLEDGE ABOUT DUNCAN'S curse, but she found it fascinating and asked him to wait while she looked through her books for information on ways that magical artifacts could be linked to people. He wore a less-than-delighted expression when she took out a magnifying glass to examine and measure his scar but waved for me to return home when I started yawning, the long night having caught up with me.

"Get some rest and something to eat," he said.

He might have heard my stomach growl earlier.

"Okay." I stepped toward the door but paused when Rue pointed at the medallion around his neck.

All except part of the chain was hidden under his shirt, but she could doubtless sense its magic.

"What is that?" she asked. "A new ornament, yes? It does not have the power to protect you from this curse?"

"If it does," Duncan said, pulling it out from under his shirt, "it's not been inclined to use it on me yet. I've even rubbed it and *asked* it to, though I don't know if there are command words that summon its power. Before, it automatically protected me from some orange beams that would have made me double over in pain. But it might only defend a person against acute threats." He looked toward me, eyebrows raised.

"I don't know." I hadn't thought to ask him about the medallion earlier but wasn't surprised he'd attempted to elicit its powers. "All Mom's medallion ever did for me was glow when I touched it. It didn't stop Radomir's goons from attacking us. Or a weirdo bipedfuris from chasing me."

Maybe I shouldn't have said that. As far as I knew, Duncan hadn't told Rue that he had old-world blood and could become a two-legged werewolf as well as a regular wolf.

But she, with her magnifying glass now pointed at the medallion, didn't seem to hear my words.

"Unlike with that case," Duncan said, "there aren't any inscriptions on it that I noticed. It does warm slightly to your touch if you sleep with it under your pillow and brush against it in the night."

"When my mom said you could borrow it, I doubt she had pillow cuddling in mind."

"I feel obligated to keep it somewhere secure."

"You don't have a safe in your van, huh?"

"Just a few strongboxes that hold magical equipment. And the glovebox."

"Where you keep your eighties cassettes?"

"Among other things, yes."

"I guess I'm glad you don't sleep with *them* under your pillow."

"They're not as irreplaceable as a magical medallion."

"Perhaps," Rue said, "if you nattered less, your magical items would have more opportunity to assist with your ailments."

I raised my eyebrows. "I thought you'd charmed her."

"With my handsome face and charismatic smile, not my words."

"Books," Rue announced, setting aside her magnifying glass and heading toward one of the many shelves in the living room. "I must spend some hours doing research. Oh, and I'd like samples of the area."

"The, uh, area?" Duncan asked.

"Around your scar. Are you afraid of needles?"

"Not at all. I even gave Luna a sword in case she desires to stab me." After the words came out, he must have remembered that the sword was currently missing—and I blamed myself for its loss—because he lifted an apologetic hand toward me.

"All mates with tendencies toward nattering should be so conscientious with their gift giving. Here." Rue returned with a wooden case that looked like it would contain chess or backgammon pieces. When she opened it, numerous antique needles and syringes lay mounted inside. "Let's take that sample."

Duncan bared his teeth but didn't step back. *I* would have.

After he'd suggested I get some sleep, I'd been halfway to the door, but I asked, "Do you want me to stay?"

"That depends," Duncan said. "Will you hold my hand and lend moral support or mock me if I shed a tear when that giant needle slides into a vein?" He pointed to one that looked like it should be applied to a horse rather than a human.

"Given my nature, it might be a little of both."

He smiled and waved me to the door. "Get some rest. I'll be fine."

"Well, don't scream. Quiet hours here start at ten."

"I'll keep your regulations in mind while I'm enduring my agony."

"You're a good werewolf." I gave him a thumbs-up before stepping out, glancing at my phone to see if Jasmine had sent any updates.

She hadn't yet. There probably weren't any images on the internet that matched the hand device. It might well have been in the back of Abrams's safe for fifty years, long pre-dating the internet.

On the way to my apartment, I picked up some garbage on the grounds and grabbed my mail. A letter from Austin at the Air Force base in Mississippi surprised me. He hadn't written anything to me on physical paper since his fifth-grade teacher had made him practice addressing letters during handwriting class.

My first thought was that it was a Christmas card that he'd mailed before flying home, but he'd come in person, so he wouldn't have sent one. Besides, this had a recent postmark.

Butterflies fluttered in my stomach as I reached for a letter opener in my kitchen junk drawer. After the night of our battle— after learning that his mother was a *werewolf*—Austin hadn't said much, giving only brief answers to questions and looking relieved to head back to the airport. I'd *wanted* to talk about it, to explain why I'd kept it a secret, but I also hadn't wanted to overload him with information he wasn't ready for. Or didn't want? Had he even known werewolves existed before that night? I didn't know.

My hands shook a little as I unfolded a yellow, lined piece of paper.

Hi, Mom.

I hope this isn't cowardly or anything, but I wasn't sure what to say if I called or texted. What I saw that night didn't make sense to me, even though I'd heard... Well, I guess I didn't believe the stories of vampires and werewolves and Santa Claus. Not since I was a little kid. It was all... really weird and confusing.

I called Cam from the airport to ask if he knew. He sounded skeptical when I blurted everything out to him and said I should have stayed off the 'shrooms. I wasn't even having a beer that night though. I tried to explain, but he said I was nuts and told me to call Dad for proof that you aren't a werewolf.

. . .

I couldn't keep from grimacing hugely at that line. Chad was such a loser that I hated any suggestions that my sons were keeping in touch with him. What if Austin *had* called? Chad knew my secret. Unfortunately. He would tell Austin what he knew.

But... that was okay, wasn't it? After that night, it wasn't as if I could hide my lupine side from my son. I didn't necessarily want to anymore, anyway. It had mainly been when they'd been children that I'd wanted them to have normal lives. And I'd done my best to be a normal *human* mother, not a paranormal weirdo that they would end up in therapy over.

I haven't called Dad yet, the letter continued. *I don't know if you know, but he's kind of weird when it comes to you.*

"Tell me about it," I muttered.

Anyway, I wanted to write to warn you that I talked to Cam. I wasn't sure if... Well, I guess you didn't *want us all to know since you never said anything, and that was also weird, but I should have talked to you before I left. Next time, I will if you want to say anything. Or if you don't, that's fine. I am... a little confused though. Does this mean I could turn into a wolf one day? Is it genetic? Like Huntington's disease or something?*

Write me back, okay? I'm kind of busy with training, and they take our phones sometimes.

Bye.

Austin

. . .

I read the letter a couple of times. A poet, my son was not, but I was glad he'd reached out. That he wanted me to reply in a similar form made me think he still didn't know what to say and didn't want to talk on the phone. But this was something. He was curious, if only about whether he'd spontaneously turn into a werewolf.

What would Cameron's response be? Would he research it further and reach out to me? Or brush it off, believing, as he'd said, Austin was nuts?

I missed my oldest son and wished he *would* reach out. If not for checking his social-media sites, I wouldn't have known what state he was in, or if he was in the country at all. We'd barely spoken these last two years. *He* would be the more likely one to call Chad. But Chad already knew, so it didn't matter, did it? As long as my ex-husband didn't show up, looking for the wolf case. He had been, after all, the one who'd originally brought it to the Seattle area and hidden it in the heat duct under my bed where it had lain dormant for months—no, *years*—until Duncan had arrived in search of it.

The memory of him smiling and whistling as he ran his metal detector over logs and leaves in the woods adjacent to Sylvan Serenity came to mind. I'd thought him terribly suspicious but also handsome. And I still thought him handsome. I wanted...

"For him *not* to die, damn it." I thought about the translation on the wolf case. *Straight from the source lies within protection from venom, poison, and the bite of the werewolf.* Too bad nothing suggested it would help with curses. The medallion might—if we could figure out how to draw upon its power. "Would Mom know more about that?"

Thus far, she hadn't known that much when it came to her medallion, just that it had been passed down from one alpha female in the pack to the next. Still, it might be worth consulting her on this. Maybe if we brought together the case with its mushroom-shaped artifact and the two medallions and the witch talisman, they would have a magical powwow again, and Duncan would get another vision. One that told him how to fix himself.

I sighed wistfully, resolving to drag Duncan up to Mom's cabin. Even if she didn't know anything helpful, the pack's wise wolf or archivist might.

It was late, but I texted Lorenzo. Since Mom didn't have a cell phone or even a land line, he was my conduit to her.

Duncan and I have some questions about the medallions and what they can do. Will you ask Mom if it's okay if we come up in the morning?

It didn't take long for an answer. *Your mother is always willing to see you and the one she hopes will become your mate.*

I just call him Duncan.

Never one to be drawn into snark and sarcasm, Lorenzo only replied with, *Umbra will be here when you come.*

Thank you.

15

I kept glancing at Duncan's forehead as I drove us through the foothills outside of Monroe and into the woodlands around my Mom's cabin. I'd picked up my truck from the shop, and it once again had both fenders and was running agreeably. Its passenger was less agreeable.

"The gouge isn't *that* deep, is it?" Duncan hid his scar with the heel of his palm. "Rue's needle was the size of a feeding tube, but the mark it left should heal quickly."

"It's fine. I'm admiring your profile."

"You're eyeing my scar like it's a viper that'll leap out at you."

"I can't help it. It concerns me. It's not glowing, the way it did when the device was trying to summon you, but it seems..."

Duncan sighed and dropped his hand. "Like an angry red welt, I know. Despite being largely oblivious to my looks and not having a touch of vanity, I do occasionally peek at myself in the mirror."

"Oblivious to your looks? Didn't you tell me you trim yourself assiduously to make sure your naked body is appealing to anyone who looks at it?"

"I prefer a tidy mien because *I* must look at it."

"But without even a touch of vanity."

"Precisely."

"Did Rue have any ideas?"

Did she have a *cure* for his curse? No. If she'd discovered anything, Duncan would have said so when I'd picked him up that morning—or he would have knocked on my door the night before. Still, I couldn't help but hope.

"Not that she mentioned, but she was *hmm*ing and *uhmm*ing when I left her apartment near midnight. She did smugly inform me, after she took her samples, that she could use the genetic material to clone me and create a Duncan of her own. I wasn't that amused."

"I'm sure she won't do that."

"Because it would be morally reprehensible to create a clone without someone's permission?"

"Well, maybe, but mostly she's pretty old to raise a test-tube baby."

"So is Abrams, but that hasn't stopped him," Duncan said grimly.

"Did you ever learn the kid's name?"

"Lykos."

"Doesn't that just mean wolf?"

"In Greek, yes. Abrams was never that original when it came to names." He waved at his chest, reminding me that Duncan was a name he'd adopted. His original name, presumably also granted by Abrams, had been Drakon, the Greek for dragon.

"Did you get to speak to him?" I asked. "Lykos?"

"Not as much as you did, I think."

"I only told him that Abrams and Radomir were bad guys, chocolate was worth trading medallions for, and that he'd rather have a salami log than pick a fight with me."

"Those are more in-depth conversations than I've had with

him. The couple of times our paths crossed, I mostly grunted at him."

"Were you a wolf or bipedfuris on those occasions?"

"Less often than you'd think, given that degree of articulation."

I glanced at him as I navigated the truck off the paved road and onto the meandering dirt route that led through the trees toward the cabin.

"I didn't know what to say," Duncan admitted. "I'm not even sure... Is he more like my son? Or my brother? Oh, logically I know we're siblings—identical twins, I suppose—but the age difference makes it confusing."

"The weird sci-fi cloning makes it confusing."

He laughed softly. "That too."

"Maybe just befriend him, if you can. We should try to get him away from those guys. Being raised in a laboratory *can't* be healthy."

"I survived it," Duncan said dryly.

"You had access to a library."

"That did help."

An oncoming SUV with *Logan's Real Estate* on the side forced me to navigate to the edge of the road, my truck's tire dipping into a deep pothole. The frame creaked in protest. The poor vehicle. It had endured a lot this winter.

The last time we'd driven up here, I'd noticed a for-sale sign on a property down the road from my mom's. Since then, a clear case containing flyers had been added. Fresh bite holes in the wood post suggested that some of my relatives were taking umbrage at the prospective sale, probably because it was undeveloped land full of trees, and their hunts took them across it often.

Surprisingly, Mom stood in the driveway when we arrived, Lorenzo at her side. Her arms were folded across her chest as she glowered toward the road. His expression was more pensive.

I rolled down the window and pulled to a stop in front of

them. "When Lorenzo said you'd be here when we arrived, I didn't expect you to greet us at the head of the driveway."

"We're scowling fearsomely to drive away that presumptuous real estate agent," Mom said.

I glanced back, remembering the SUV but nothing remarkable about the driver.

"Did you show him your canines? Your *lupines*?" I asked. "That always helps."

"Lorenzo did."

"As your mother commanded." He inclined his head. "I am, of course, here to protect her."

"To mundane outsiders, he's more fearsome than the magical alarms." Mom tilted her head toward the ferns between the trees along the winding gravel driveway.

Having felt how effective those magical security devices could be, I curled my lip in that direction. I would rather face Lorenzo.

They stepped to the side so we could drive up to the cabin and park. I offered a ride in the truck bed—in his wolf form, Lorenzo had hopped back there before—but maybe Mom was past the age of wanting to clamber over tailgates. Holding hands, they walked up the driveway after we passed.

"What did the real estate agent want?" I asked when we all stood on the porch.

Mom's gaze drifted to the medallion under Duncan's shirt, but she nodded, looking satisfied that he wore it, not annoyed that he'd asked to borrow it. She'd offered him a place in the pack, and maybe she believed that he would accept it, and the medallion would soon hang again on the neck of a male Snohomish Savager.

"To see our land." Mom waved at her cabin but also the surrounding forest.

I didn't know how many acres came with the property. It wasn't the home I'd grown up in, which had burned to the ground in a fire, and I'd never poked around in the county records to find out where Mom's land ended and other parcels began. Werewolves weren't ones to erect fences. Someone had mentioned that the property abutted state land to the rear, but I didn't know if the gully with the magical cave lay within her borders or not.

"Does he want to list it?" I asked.

Mom's lips rippled. "He said it *is* listed and that he has interested clients."

"Uh, I assume you didn't do that."

"I most certainly did not. This land has belonged to the pack for generations." Mom said *the pack* but touched her chest. Presumably, it belonged to her. Others in the family had nearby properties, and when the pack was in wolf form, they tended to come and go on their hunts without worrying about who owned what. "I've talked to Renata, and she's going to check on it."

That was Jasmine's mom, and I nodded since she was in the real estate business. She would be able to get to the bottom of the problem.

"Apparently," Lorenzo said, "it's not that uncommon for crooks to list land they don't own in the hope that they'll be able to make a quick cash deal with someone willing to skip going through a title agency. That's usually *raw* land, not a parcel with a home on it, but..." He waved around the area, as if to say the rural location made it susceptible.

"A *competent* agent," Mom said, "would do some research to make sure someone has the right to sell a property before listing it."

"Hm." I couldn't help but wonder if Radomir and Abrams were behind this, scheming to sell Mom's property out from under her. That seemed like a lot of work—*criminal* work—just to get her medallion, but they were posing as buyers for Sylvan Serenity, so who knew what ends they would go to in order to disrupt our lives and get what they wanted.

"Renata said she knows what to do to get the listing removed, and that I don't need to personally show up at the office of the real estate agent who put it up." Mom lifted her hand, fingers curled to emulate claws digging someone's eyes out.

"You sound disappointed that you don't need to do that," Lorenzo said.

"No, I'm too tired to want to drive around and threaten people." She sighed. Sadly.

My throat tightened in sympathy.

"Perhaps that's the part that's disappointing to you," he murmured, wrapping an arm around her shoulders.

"I do miss having vigor." Mom looked from Duncan to me.

My sympathy waned as I had the feeling she would use that as a segue to ask if we were frolicking between the sheets to make young werewolf pups.

"We have a problem, Mom," I blurted, hoping to forestall that discussion. "Duncan might be dying."

His eyebrows arched. Maybe I shouldn't have been so blunt.

From the way Mom's lips twisted, I expected her to say something like, *Join the club.*

"What happened?" she asked instead, perhaps remembering that she wanted him to father offspring with me. That would be hard for him to accomplish if he was dead.

I summarized the night of the battle, reluctantly admitting that I'd been the one to destroy the control device. She'd been the one to suggest I do that—well, we'd discussed *stealing* it—but I didn't try to put any blame on her. I'd had an inkling that destroying it wouldn't end well, but I'd been the one to snap it in half with my own jaws.

"The medallion protected you from its control?" Mom asked Duncan when I finished.

"It did." He rested his hand on it. "I didn't know that would happen when I went looking for it. I'd hoped to help Luna and your family by finding it and returning it to you."

"Assuming you could break Radomir's control and not return it to *him*?" I asked.

"You know that was my desire."

"Yeah, but he was also the reason you were hunting for it in the first place."

"Something I've not denied." Duncan bowed to me, though he glanced at Lorenzo, who smiled slightly.

"Women may forgive you your transgressions," Lorenzo said, "but they'll never forget them."

"I've observed that to be true," Duncan said.

I exchanged looks with Mom, whose lips were twisting again, though her gaze soon returned to the medallion. Today, it lay on Duncan's button-down shirt, gleaming in the sun but not glowing and emanating power the way it had during the battle.

"It is interesting that it would protect you from the magic of that control device when it existed," Mom said, "but cannot do so after it's gone."

"Inconvenient more than interesting," Duncan murmured.

"Is it that it *can*not?" Lorenzo asked. "Or perhaps that it *will* not?"

"What are you suggesting?" Mom asked him.

Lorenzo shrugged. "It's your family's heirloom. They both are, right?" He nodded toward the cabin, where Mom probably had the matching medallion in her bedside table.

"They haven't always belonged to my direct ancestors but always to the Snohomish Savagers, originally the Sardegna Savagers. Or *selvaggio*, I believe it was. I never learned the tongue. The pack left Italia several generations ago." Mom lifted a finger, stepped inside, and returned with her medallion.

With a fanged wolf in profile in the center, it was almost identical to Duncan's, but the head engraved on hers had smaller and narrower features. More petite, to suggest a female wolf? Long

ago, maybe an actual male and female alpha had been the inspira-
tion and posed for the engravings.

"I brought the wolf case and witch talisman along." I waved to
the truck. "I thought having them all together again might do
something. Like last time."

By *do something*, I meant cure Duncan.

Crossing my mental fingers, I hopped off the porch and pulled
the items out of the glovebox. I hadn't brought an oven mitt or ski
glove, and the case zapped me painfully.

"Aren't we friends yet?" I grumbled, enduring the punishment
long enough to rest it on the porch railing. I put the talisman next
to it.

Lorenzo watched all this curiously. Mom merely nodded. She
wouldn't know about the vision Duncan had received, but she'd
been there when the case had opened. In addition to healing her
poisoned cut, the mushroom-shaped artifact inside had magneti-
cally or magically drawn the other artifacts toward it.

"You may need to turn into the bipedfuris again to get the case
to open," I told Duncan.

Eager barks and a howl came from the woods behind the
property, and he looked in that direction instead of answering.

"Is the family on a hunt?" I guessed, though it was full
daylight, no hint of the moon in the sky.

"Sort of," Mom said with an eye roll. "There are yellow-bellied
marmots in a rocky area back there by some old mine shafts. Gold
prospectors poked around in the hills along the stream there in
the 1800s, before our family purchased the property. The marmots
love the area. It's got water and rocks and holes and whatever they
like to eat. A couple of them have come out of hibernation early
and are taunting predators with cheeping sounds. Emilio and his
brother are back there, digging at the rocks. They consider it fun. I
think they're idiots."

"You'd better get things straightened out with the real estate agent," I said, "so you don't lose land filled with such valuable resources."

"If you're talking about the mineral rights, I don't think anyone ever found much gold back there."

"I meant the marmots. Keeping young werewolves entertained is important."

"Ginevra's boys *did* play back there when they were kids," Mom said. "It's a great spot for youths."

More eager barks and yips wafted to us.

"And the pathologically immature," she added.

I snorted and looked toward Duncan again. He was gripping his chin and studying the case.

"*Can* you still call upon the bipedfuris?" I asked softly, stepping close to him. "Or is it harder now that you're..." I waved vaguely, not wanting to suggest he was weakened or diminished.

"I'm still fine," he said dryly.

"Then there won't be a problem changing to prompt the case to open?"

"I wish we'd brought some rattlesnakes."

"We still don't know if waving a venomous reptile over the case will also cause it to open."

"Because we keep forgetting to try." Duncan pushed a hand through his hair. "I haven't turned into the bipedfuris since the battle at the cabin. I'm not sure if I should."

"They don't have another way to compel or manipulate you in that form, right?" I recalled that he'd been more susceptible to the control device as the bipedfuris.

"Oh, I certainly hope not."

"But you're not sure?" I raised my eyebrows.

"I didn't see any evidence that they had a back-up device or anything of that ilk. But I'm a little... gun-shy, I suppose."

"I haven't noticed that you're any kind of shy."

"I have my moments." Duncan glanced at Mom.

She and Lorenzo had stepped back to give us privacy but were watching, no doubt curious about what would happen when the case opened again.

"The artifact inside has healed me, but it's also... I'm not sure how to explain it. Both times I've been the bipedfuris when that lid has opened, I've felt hatred from it. That it wants me dead. The first time, I was so busy fighting that I barely registered it. I even forgot about it until I felt it again." He tilted his head toward the cabin.

"When you turned to see if it would help Mom."

The artifact *had* helped her, but not in the way I'd hoped. It had healed the wound she'd received from a bear trap, not her cancer, or The Taint, as the wise wolf called it.

"Yes," Duncan said.

"When you were pacing around and grabbing your forehead, I thought you were agitated because the control device had been activated, that Radomir was trying to summon you."

"Oh, I did feel that, but I also felt hatred rippling from the glowing artifact inside." He eyed the case.

"I suppose that's not surprising. It was made to protect people from werewolf bites, among other things. Do you think that's why it zaps me every time I pick it up? Warning me that it's not for us?"

"Maybe."

"I should ask Bolin if it zaps him."

He and his father had studied it when we'd first unearthed it.

"I'd assumed that was a defensive mechanism and that it zaps *everyone*," I added.

"I don't know."

"It did help you before though." I pointed at the medallion, though it had been my mother's medallion that had been involved that day. "Giving you the vision so you could find it."

"*That* helped me." Duncan pointed toward Mom's medallion. "I think *that*—" he shifted his pointing finger to the case without making contact, "—was the catalyst. Its magic and magnetism woke up the medallion, but I don't think *it* cared about helping me."

"It *cured* you when you were poisoned during the fight with Augustus," I said. "And it healed Mom's poisoned wound too."

"Maybe its programming to heal cuts lined with poison overrides its distaste for werewolves," he said.

"It could also only feel distaste for werewolves when they're in one of their furry forms," Mom, who'd been listening in, suggested.

"Or the bipedfuris form specifically." I nodded. "That's the only time a werewolf is in danger of spreading lycanthropy through its bite. The translation specifically mentioned protecting against that. One does wonder, if our kind aren't meant to have it, why the case has ended up here though."

Mom shrugged. "Happenstance, I imagine. You said your ex-husband found it, didn't you?"

"Yeah, but that wasn't..." I paused. I'd had visions that had suggested the artifact or some other magical or maybe even divine force had orchestrated that, but did I want to admit that? In front of my mother? "I'm not sure that was only chance," I said with a shrug.

"What else would it be?" Mom squinted at me.

Thinking I was nuts? Or would she not bat an eye at talk of visions? She'd mentioned the magical cave and sent me to it, so maybe she'd experienced such things herself.

"I'll give it a try." Duncan, eyes focused on the case as he wrestled with his own doubts, might or might not have been listening to us. "But if I turn furry, then run off into the woods yipping, you'll know it's doing something to me."

"Or maybe I'll think you're being drawn by squeaking marmots," I said as a few more barks drifted to us.

What kind of wolves *barked* like that? They sounded like mindless dogs.

"Well, one does enjoy a hunt, though I prefer larger and more dangerous game." Duncan smiled faintly, but it didn't reach his eyes. Because he thought turning into the bipedfuris while near the case again was a bad idea?

"You don't have to do it," I said. "We can try other things. Maybe Rue will come up with something. Or want to study you further."

"Save me from that," Duncan murmured, then stepped back and started removing his clothing. "It's my life that's in the balance. I'd better try anything we can think of to save it."

"Okay." I didn't suggest he might be open to trying anything he could think of to avoid spending more time being scrutinized by an alchemist with giant needles and syringes.

Leaving only the medallion on, Duncan draped his clothing on the railing. Then he gripped the wolf head, looking off into the woods as he did whatever mental tricks were necessary to convince his savage side to come forth without the moon's call.

It might have been another round of yips from the woods that did it, a promise of lupine fun to be had if one came to the marmot area. Duncan grew broader and taller, fur sprouting as his limbs thickened and fingernails and toenails turned into claws.

The lid on the case flew open, intense light shining out, as it had before in this situation. Growling, Duncan took several steps back from it, arms spreading, clawed fingers flexing. The talisman, still lying on the railing, skidded toward the case, only stopping when it clunked against it. The chain around Duncan's neck lifted into the air, also pulled in that direction. Mom's medallion shifted in her hand. Only her grip kept it from flying over to attach itself to the side of the case—or the glowing artifact inside.

All four of us stood still, only Duncan shifting and growling. Feeling the artifact's agitation, as he'd described it, toward him?

I didn't feel anything like that, but I did sense the great magical power emanating from it. I crossed my fingers, hoping it could do something to help. All this power and magic *had* to be able to break a curse, right?

Despite their attraction toward the artifact, the medallions didn't glow themselves. Nor did I receive any visions. Would it help if I touched one?

I lifted a finger toward Mom's medallion, thinking to try, but Duncan swayed, arms spreading, as if he was trying to retain his balance.

"Are you okay?" I asked.

The bipedfuris bared his teeth in a grimace and swayed again. There weren't any magical beams lancing toward him—no attacks of any kind that I could detect—but he looked like he was in pain. Then he crumpled, landing on his side on the wooden porch.

Alarmed, I sprang toward Duncan, kneeling and touching him. I glanced at the case, afraid the artifact was attacking him in some way I couldn't sense. It continued to glow, but it didn't do anything more threatening.

"Duncan?" I touched his furred torso.

His eyes closed, as if in sleep. Or in death. The thought scaring me, I shifted my fingers to his throat to search for his pulse.

His heart was still beating—that was something, anyway—but he didn't stir at my touch. He lay unresponsive.

16

"What happened to him?" Mom asked.

My hand on Duncan's furred chest, I shook my head. "I don't know."

The medallion remained raised from his torso. If not for its chain, it would have been pulled to the artifact.

I wrapped my hand around the medallion, as if it might have answers.

It pulsed warmly in my grip, and words floated through my mind. *Not for you.*

I blinked.

Had it *spoken* to me?

What? I thought at it.

Not for you. An image came with the words. It showed my mother's medallion, the female version.

Of course. That made sense. But...

Are you for Duncan? I mentally asked.

Not for you.

Yeah, I got that.

The medallion didn't share any more words. I half-wondered if it was my imagination.

"Are you for Duncan?" I tried repeating the words aloud as well as in my mind.

Behind me, Mom and Lorenzo stirred, probably wondering who I was talking to since Duncan's eyes remained closed.

A sense of uncertainty emanated from the medallion.

"You don't know yet?" I asked. "Because he's not one of the Savagers? He's been invited in, you know. He's still thinking about it. Can you lift the curse that's killing him?"

It was a lot to ask a magical artifact, and I wasn't surprised when I didn't get an answer beyond its lingering uncertainty. Other times, I'd sensed emotion from the mushroom-shaped artifact, but this was the first hint that the medallions had a sentience or whatever one might call this.

The magical aura that was always present around Duncan rippled to my senses, and I lifted my hand. Without opening his eyes or stirring in any way, his body transformed. Soon, he lay unconscious as a man again.

Still nestled in its case on the railing, the artifact ceased glowing. The uncertainty I'd sensed from the medallion faded, as did most of the magic it radiated. It was as if it had gone dormant. The medallions and talisman also slumped, gravity retaking them as they were no longer drawn to the artifact. The lid on the case remained open, but the pull had faded.

"That was less enlightening than I hoped." I couldn't help but feel we'd wasted our time by coming up here. If Duncan didn't wake up, we would have *more* than wasted our time.

"Maybe I erred in my choice," Mom said.

"About what?" I asked.

She pointed at Duncan.

What did she refer to? Not his suitability as my mate, surely. Unless she sensed that he was in a weakened state now and rejected him on those grounds. I gritted my teeth at the thought. This was *temporary*, damn it.

"What do you mean?" I asked tensely, ready to snap if she voiced my thoughts.

"The medallion doesn't seem sure about him," she said. "Didn't you sense that?"

"I sensed... uncertainty." That was the word that had kept floating through my mind.

"Yes, exactly. When I invited him into the pack and to mate with you, it didn't occur to me that the medallion would object to him. I didn't even know the medallions could do that."

My first response was to bristle again about the *mating* talk, but that wasn't important right now.

"You think it's not lifting the curse because it doesn't know if he's worthy?" I asked, not sure I followed her thoughts.

Mom spread her arms. "I gave him much credit because of his old-world power, but..."

"He's *completely* worthy," I snapped. "Of anything. And it has nothing to do with his power."

She looked at me like she'd birthed a simpleton.

I surged to my feet, fists clenching, though what I planned to do with my fists, I didn't know. I couldn't punch my old, sick mother. But frustration boiled inside of me. I'd wanted this to be the answer, to save Duncan's life.

"If there's anything wrong with him or his *power* in the eyes of a piece of jewelry, it's only because that curse is weakening him." No, it was *killing* him. I swallowed around my tight throat. "It should fix him, and then it would see that he's worthy."

Mom opened her mouth, maybe to say that the medallion didn't have the *power* to fix the curse.

"I'm not worthy *yet*," came a croak from below before she could speak.

"Duncan." I knelt and rested a hand on his chest again.

"Ah, lovely." He clasped his hand over mine. "A sick man should be fondled."

"What happened? Did the artifact attack you?"

"I believe I, ahem." He eyed Mom and Lorenzo before lowering his voice to a whisper. "I believe I fainted."

"You... fainted?" I asked slowly.

"Perhaps Americans would say *passed out*. In a manly manner."

"We would say that, but it had to do with the artifact, right? I didn't sense it attack you, but you wouldn't faint in the middle of the day for no reason."

His expression bleak, he met my eyes. "I have been feeling a touch dizzy and lightheaded now and then. Since the fight last night. I'm afraid my condition is progressing."

"That's alarming, but it had to have been something to do with the magic."

"Perhaps so." Duncan glanced at Mom and Lorenzo again.

They weren't staring at him with condemnation and judgment, but I suspected Duncan would have preferred fewer witnesses for, as he'd put it, the progression of his condition.

"What did you mean when you said you're not worthy yet?" I asked.

"That's the impression I got from the medallion when... Well, I silently asked it to help me. If it could." He looked sheepish.

"I asked it the same thing," I said.

"It gave me a vibe of... Well, it seemed to imply that it *could* help me if I proved myself worthy of its help. Of *it*."

"These medallions were designed to be worn by the alphas of the pack." Mom clearly had no trouble following the conversation even though Duncan had lowered his voice.

"And I'm not part of the pack. Or an alpha."

"I did offer you a place with the Savagers if you wish it," Mom said, though she looked at me, as if the decision would have been up to me.

As if I controlled Duncan. Maybe she meant that I would have to offer myself to him if we wanted him to desire to join us. There was some truth to that, I supposed. It wasn't as if any of the rest of the family had done anything to endear the Savagers to Duncan. My *cousins* had been trying to kill him.

"I do appreciate that." Duncan pushed himself to a sitting position, though he winced. Did he have a headache lingering as well as the dizziness? "I think, however, that worth has to be proven, not given." He tapped the medallion. "It's quiescent now. It's no longer responding in any way when I think words at it." He looked toward the case, the lid still open but the artifact inside dormant. "That must enhance the capabilities of other magical tools around it."

"It does... something." I shrugged, feeling helpless. "How are you supposed to prove yourself when you're..." Dying, I thought but didn't say. "Fainting?"

"It might be difficult. I've yet to defeat an enemy by fainting at his or her feet."

"No, bad guys are rarely intimidated by that."

"One might be discombobulated by it."

"*I'm* discombobulated by it. *Duncan*," I said in exasperation, though it wasn't his fault. None of this was. I slumped, and my next, "Duncan," came out softer, regret and guilt heavy on my tongue.

"We'll figure something out." He reached up and patted me.

Why was *he* the one doing the consoling? I needed to be a better person. *I* was the one who ought to be proving myself.

"You know I like a challenge," he added.

"I do know that."

Mom leaned against Lorenzo and nodded for him to guide her inside. Reminded that she was also dying, I stared at the wooden porch boards. Would the moon take everyone I cared about from me this winter? I was glad Austin was safe halfway across the country, hopefully well out of the reach of my enemies—and the bad-mojo vibe that I seemed to be emitting these days.

A text came in on my phone. Bolin.

I tried calling but got dumped straight to voicemail.

Yes, the reception out here was horrible. From the time stamp, it looked like Bolin had texted a while ago.

The buyers, it continued, *sent a building inspector over to check the apartments as part of the purchase. There's nothing unusual about that, but he looks more like he's snooping than inspecting. He asked if I had a key to your apartment specifically. I told him no, but you might want to get back here.*

I rubbed my face. If the "buyers" hadn't been Radomir and Abrams, I would have ignored the suggestion. Duncan's health was more important than my duties as a property manager. But maybe we would get lucky and those two would be in the area, waiting to pounce if their so-called building inspector found any of the artifacts they were salivating over.

"Guess it's a good thing they're all with us," I muttered.

"Hm?" Duncan prompted.

"We need to go back to Sylvan Serenity." I showed him the text. "If Radomir and Abrams are there, we're going to wring their necks until they tell us how to lift this curse."

It had better be possible.

"I don't know if I have the strength to wring any necks today." Duncan used the railing to help rise to his feet.

"You can faint on them as a distraction. Then I'll spring upon them from behind and handle the wringing."

"That would be quite thoughtful of you."

"I'm a thoughtful gal."

"Hence my adoration." Duncan smiled at me.

I tried to feel flattered, but I mostly worried for him and wanted to cry.

17

By the time we returned to Sylvan Serenity, I thought the building inspector would be gone, but Bolin was leaning against his SUV with his arms folded across his chest. A van with a removable sign stuck on the door that read *H&C Inspections* was parked next to him in *my* spot.

"Presumptuous bastard," I said.

Was that sign even legitimate? The guy had probably made it at a print shop on the way here.

Duncan looked over at me.

"The supposed inspector is in my spot." I pointed.

There were only two reserved places for staff, and Bolin had the other one.

"Will you have him towed?"

Oh, hell, wouldn't that be magnificent? I smiled with wicked glee at the thought.

"Is that the expression you wear whenever you contemplate having *my* vehicle towed?" Duncan asked.

"Absolutely." I parked a few spots away. At least it was the middle of the day so most of the lot was open. "I'm going to go pound on this guy if he's anywhere near my apartment. Will you stay here and guard the artifacts?"

"You don't want help with the pounding?"

"Not unless Radomir and Abrams are here with him. Then we'll enact our plan."

"Of me fainting on them as a distraction?" His mouth twisted with distaste. After a lifetime of being fit and virile, he had to hate losing his strength.

"Yup." I opened the door. "You can practice while I'm gone."

"How does one practice fainting?"

"I believe it involves naps."

"This is a dreadful situation."

"I could bring you a pillow."

Duncan scowled at me as I slid out.

"What's he doing now?" I asked Bolin when I joined him, pausing to peek in the van's window.

"He's supposedly inspecting the roof," Bolin said, "but he's got equipment for scoping drains with him. He *said* it was for the gutters, but he's up there poking things into the vents."

A jacket and a couple of toolboxes were all I could see in the van. Tinted back windows hid the rest of its contents.

"Let me guess," I said. "He's on the roof above *my* apartment."

"He is indeed." Bolin slanted me a long look. "He's been here all morning. I haven't seen him *inspect* any of the other buildings. I've been tempted to call my parents, but the real estate agents did connect and arrange this appointment. As far as *they* know, it's legitimate."

"Did you look this guy up? Is he a real inspector? Or someone Radomir personally picked out and had a sign and card made for?"

"He does have a business license, yes, and a website and reviews on Yelp." Bolin shrugged. "He can be legitimate but also taking a special, questionable side gig. I'm suspicious of his inspection methodology. Earlier, he looked like he might have been contemplating forcing his way into your apartment, but I've been watching him all morning. Every time he's spotted me, he's started whistling and doing something else. He is *not* a professional snoop."

"I appreciate you keeping an eye on him. Fortunately, there's nothing but espresso and chocolate in my apartment for him to find. Not that I want his grubby mitts on my caffeine supply."

"I wouldn't."

"Have you seen Radomir or Abrams?" Maybe I shouldn't have fantasized about neck-wringing, but the easiest way to find a solution to Duncan's curse would be the direct way. Abrams was the one I really needed. Radomir probably didn't know anything about how the link Abrams had long ago established between Duncan and the device worked.

"No. The buyers' real estate agent arranged this."

"I'm sure the real estate agent doesn't know anything about what Radomir and Abrams are really up to."

Bolin looked at me. "Do *you*?"

"This, I think." I waved at the inspector—he'd come into view, climbing over the apex of the roof. He looked in our direction, then dropped to his hands and knees and crawled back out of view on the far side. "Finding ways to search for the artifacts they think I have. Radomir has to be grumpy that Duncan located the one they had him looking for, only to escape with it around his neck."

"This is... an elaborate ruse only to steal something."

"Well, they don't know where the artifacts are. This gives them a way to have the premises searched."

"Do you have them with you? Or did you stash them out in the woods somewhere? I noticed someone who wasn't Duncan out there with a metal detector this morning."

"Was it a metal detector or a *magic* detector?"

"I... am not well versed enough in paranormal equipment to be certain. He was too far away for me to tell if it... had a vibe."

"A vibe? Like an aura?"

"Yes."

"Maybe you should chat up our ghost-hunting tenants to learn how to identify paranormal devices by more than vibes."

"I attempted to *chat up* one of them when they first arrived. We discovered we had few common interests."

I took that to mean they'd ignored his attempts to flirt. After making sure the inspector couldn't see us, I grabbed the case out of my truck.

Duncan had taken my advice and had his eyes closed. Napping, I assumed. Not fainting.

"How's Jasmine doing?" Bolin asked when I returned. "She didn't mention if she found the networking event fruitful. I was hoping she would call."

And that they could chat for hours about their common interests? I gave him a sympathetic smile.

"She did speak with me for a while *during* the event," he continued. "Before you, uhm, before all those fight sounds came from MacGregor's bedroom. She said her mocktail was a little weird and gave me a sip. I agreed. I should have suggested an espresso martini, though I don't know how one without alcohol might be made. Was she not drinking because she was the driver or because she prefers not to?"

"I'm not sure. Touch this, will you?"

Bolin reached out a finger. Judging by the bracing grimace he wore, he expected it to zap him. But when he touched the case, he didn't immediately pull back.

"Oh, it's not trying to electrocute people anymore?"

"It is if you're a werewolf."

"Before, it gave me a zinger every time I moved it without insulation."

"And it's not now?" I arched my eyebrows.

"Nope. What changed? The fact that you've used the artifact inside a couple of times?"

"I don't know. Nothing has changed about its relationship with me."

Bolin poked the case on a couple of different sides. "It doesn't seem to mind me anymore."

"Maybe *you've* changed. The case was made by druids, right? Maybe you're getting more druidly."

He started to snort but paused, raising a finger. "I *have* been practicing spells and more frequently making magical items."

"The bath bombs." I nodded.

"The Orbs of Entanglement." Bolin scowled at me. "When Jasmine and I charged into the back of that cabin, I threw one, bumped my elbow, and it rolled uselessly under a sofa. But then I thought about it expanding its reach and tried to *will* my power to make it do so. Surprisingly, it did. It swept out from under the couch, and one of the thugs got stuck in it." He shrugged. "It was a small use of power, but it seemed... like it meant something. Like if I kept practicing, maybe I could actually be a decent druid."

"Of course you could. I'm surprised Jasmine hasn't been more wowed by your powerful aura." I smiled, only partially sarcastic. He wasn't the stuff of most women's fantasies, but he was a good guy.

"By then, she was already a wolf. I'm not sure she saw me applying my power. Also, I tripped over a boot warmer as we charged in. It wasn't my fault—I was really startled when Jasmine turned into a wolf right in front of me. I'd known she could, but I'd never seen someone do that. Anyway, I almost landed face-first on the floor." Bolin sighed. "I'd been hoping that we would bond through fighting together, but... I almost stepped on her tail as I was flailing for balance."

"Maybe you need another battle to better show off your abilities and find your teamwork groove."

"I'm more of a lover than a fighter."

"Don't forget violinist."

"Oh, I haven't. I have many non-martial skills." Bolin tapped his chin. "I bet I could find a recipe and make her a non-alcoholic espresso martini."

"Of course you could. That's a lot easier than mastering a violin piece. I'm sure of it."

Bolin looked encouraged.

The inspector walked back into view on the roof, and I tucked the case behind my back. When he headed for the ladder, I jogged it back to my truck, returning it to the glove compartment. Duncan raised an eyebrow but didn't ask for an explanation. Maybe he'd seen Bolin's experimental pokes.

The inspector headed toward the parking lot, bringing his ladder and a toolbox with him.

"I'll be curious to see his report," Bolin said, "if the real estate agent sends a copy to us."

"Is that likely?" Despite years as a property manager, I hadn't been involved in the sale of any real estate. Not yet anyway. "One day," I vowed under my breath.

"I don't think they have to, but if they want my parents to pay for any repairs, they should send it along as proof that they're needed."

"How far will Abrams and Radomir take this charade?" I gazed out to the street, still hoping they would turn up in the area.

Duncan had left my truck and was strolling along the edge of the property. Had he spotted someone? He was looking about, maybe also hoping to find Abrams or Radomir lurking.

The inspector had almost reached us, and Bolin didn't answer my question.

When I not only saw but *sensed* the guy's approach, I

twitched in surprise. Radomir and Abrams had found a building inspector with paranormal blood. I couldn't tell if he had the tendencies of a wizard or just a clairvoyant, but, either way, if he'd gotten close to any of the artifacts, he would have sensed them.

Hell, he might sense them here if he walked past my truck. That thought sent me trotting up to the inspector, hoping to keep him from nearing my vehicle. Now I wished there *hadn't* been an open parking spot so close to the reserved staff area.

"Hi," I said when he paused, his eyebrows raised.

With the ladder under his arm, he looked like he wanted to hurry straight to his van.

"I'm Luna Valens, the property manager. The owners said I should see if you need help with anything."

The owners hadn't said anything of the sort, but when I glanced at Bolin, he didn't object. As the son of the owners, he had to count as their proxy, right?

"Move the case out of my truck," I tried to mouth to him.

Bolin squinted, not catching the words. Did he not sense that this guy had magical blood?

"I've about finished my inspection," our visitor said. "Unless you'd like to tell me about any *unusual* aspects to the property that weren't readily apparent."

"There's nothing unusual here." I smiled at him.

"That's not what the newspapers have suggested." He shifted his weight, adjusting the ladder, and tried to step past me.

Though I couldn't blame him for wanting to put away the awkward load, I blocked him and lifted a hand. "What kind of *unusual* aspects did you expect to find? Anything I should keep an eye out for? Anything we'll need to address before the sale?" I slid my phone out to text Duncan as I tilted my chin toward the closest building. "It hasn't been long since I cleaned the roofs and the gutters, but the water from the downspouts does tend to pool around the foundations during a heavy rain. I was thinking of getting some extenders."

The inspector followed my gaze, but he seemed to be looking at the bushes and hedges along the walkways and near the walls of the buildings. Wondering if I'd *buried* the artifacts out here?

Will you move the case out of the truck when this guy isn't looking? I sent the text to Duncan and wished he'd stayed in the truck, napping.

"I was going to mention that in my report," the inspector said absently, then eyed me.

Could he tell I was a werewolf? And did he look a little nervous? Maybe. He didn't try to pass me again, but he shifted his grip on the ladder, like he might club me with it.

Instead, he looked toward the woods, and relief spilled out of him. "There's my assistant."

A shaggy man with a metal detector walked out of the woods, shaking his head. He was lean, almost gangly, but also had a paranormal vibe, a stronger one that I could sense from a greater distance.

I almost gaped, realizing it was a *feral* paranormal vibe. He was a werewolf. Not one I recognized, but there were lone wolves in the city, men and women who avoided the Savagers and the other packs to the south of Seattle.

"Your assistant was... inspecting the woods?" I scratched my jaw, looking around for Duncan. Had he gotten my text? Now that I needed him, I didn't see him anywhere. By the moon, I hoped he hadn't passed out behind a bush somewhere. "The property ends with the lawn there."

"Those woods have been interesting to a lot of parties," Bolin said quietly.

"Only duplicitous parties with nefarious intent," I muttered.

"Didn't we originally meet Duncan sniffing around back there?"

"I stand by my statement."

The inspector straightened, appearing bolstered by the approach of his ally. He took a step around me, and I shifted, wanting to block him again. I groped for something to ask to distract him.

His head snapped up, his eyes focusing not on me but on my truck. Damn it. He'd sensed the artifact.

"Do you—" I started.

He swung the ladder at me.

I saw it coming and caught it, my strength a match for his, but his buddy charged across the lawn toward us.

My skin flushed, nerves sending pricks of magic through my body, the change attempting to take me. But cars were driving by in the street, and a tenant might pull into the parking lot at any moment. I fought down the magic, not wanting any more witnesses to see me change. Too many people already knew what I could become.

"Look out, Luna." Bolin stepped back and delved into his man purse for who knew what.

His warning was about the approaching werewolf, but the inspector lowered the ladder and threw a punch at me. Ducking it, I yanked the ladder away from him. I backed up and swung, trying to hit him with it at the same time as I chucked it onto the lawn. It clipped his arm, and he stumbled back, then scrambled farther away.

Bolin threw something into the grass at the werewolf's feet. Green smoke wafted up. The guy, eyes savage even though he hadn't shifted forms yet, leaped through it and rushed at me.

The inspector was circling behind the bushes, trying to reach the parking lot from another direction. He wanted to get around me, not fight me.

"Keep him away from my truck," I barked at Bolin, crouching

to deal with the werewolf. He sprang over the ladder and reached for me.

As I dodged his grasp, I again struggled to keep my wolf from rising. Unfortunately, I didn't have a powerful weapon to use in my human form.

"Really need to find that sword." After avoiding the man's grasping hands, I sprang upon the ladder and hefted it.

I spun with it in my grip. The werewolf turned to rush me again. I slammed the ladder into his side with more than typical human strength, but it didn't faze him. He dove, trying to tackle me to the ground. I dodged to the side and kicked. He was fast and might have caught me, but my foot dove into his stomach. He grunted and pitched forward. I kicked him again, heel slamming into his hip. It unbalanced him enough that he dropped to his knees.

I leaped onto his back, hoping to pin him.

A grunt came from the parking lot, then the thump of something hitting the side of my truck.

"Get out of the way, you stupid kid. I— What the hell is that?"

The man under my knees heaved upright, letting out a snarl that was more animal than human. He had to be on the verge of changing himself.

Unbalanced, I pitched to the side, but I kicked out as I hit the grass, hoping to keep him from springing upon me. He spun toward me, grasping, but my heel clipped him in the jaw. His head snapped back. Thrusting up from the ground, I kicked again and connected solidly. He tumbled to the side.

I rolled over and leaped after him, punching him twice before he could recover. The blows made my knuckles smart, but magic and irritation gave me the strength to ignore the pain. Again, I pinned the guy, this time wrapping my hands around his throat to convince him to stay down.

"Get off my property, or I'll break your neck." I squeezed while

voicing the threat, hoping he recognized what I was and understood that I could kill him.

When he stilled, taking me seriously, I risked glancing toward
the parking lot.

Bolin's man purse swung through the air on its strap, the bag
clubbing the inspector in the head. The man was backed up
against my truck, a green vine wrapped around his ankle. It
extended out of the pavement between the tires.

"There's a feature I didn't know my truck had," I muttered.

"Quit hitting me, kid." The inspector managed to snatch the
bag and stop it from landing again.

He yanked a multitool from a belt holder and flicked open a
knife, then used the blade to cut the strap on Bolin's bag. He
crouched down to hack at the vine, trying to get it to release his
ankle.

"That's a Stefano Ricci," Bolin yelled, then clubbed the guy
several more times, both with his fist and the bag. "You don't *cut*
the leather."

Enduring the blows, the inspector focused on the vine until he
sawed through it and could jump upright again. He grabbed Bolin
and lifted the knife. Shit.

I released the werewolf and ran over to help my intern. A surge
of power came from Bolin, flaring like a sun to my senses, and he
leaped back quickly enough to avoid the knife swipe. At the same
time, another vine snaked out from under the truck. It rose into
the air and swatted the inspector's hand with a hard smack. He
dropped the multitool and saw me coming. Cursing, he ran
around the back of the truck and sprinted to his van.

The werewolf, red marks around his neck, glanced at me, then
also rushed to the van.

"Did they get into my truck?" I crouched, planning to charge
after them if they had, but the doors were shut, the locks
engaged.

"My bag!" Bolin held it up, waving it to emphasize the severed strap.

A familiar hatchback rolled down our lane of the parking lot, and he jerked it down, not complaining further. That was Jasmine's car.

Even as she headed toward us, the van drove straight toward her.

I sprinted after it, but what could I do to stop a van? Even as a werewolf, I didn't have the strength to halt a two-ton automobile.

Jasmine saw the threat and swerved to the side, but there wasn't enough room for her car to squeeze past the van. It would hit her before I reached it.

Scant feet ahead of me, a vine sprouted from the pavement. As thick as my wrist, it shot out and wrapped around the van's back fender. The vehicle halted, tires squealing as it tried and failed to continue forward. The engine revved, the driver glancing in a side mirror.

Behind me, Bolin had stepped into the lane and stood, fists clenched, his face full of concentration. The vine stretched but didn't snap, didn't give in the least.

Jasmine had time to back her hatchback out of the lane and into another, one well out of the van's path. Sweat rolled down the side of Bolin's face.

I started toward the driver's side of the van, intending to yank the inspector out, but the vine released abruptly. It disappeared into the pavement as fast as it had appeared.

Released from its druidic imprisonment, the van rolled over a curb, thunked down, then zipped away. It peeled out of the parking lot with impressive speed, leaving the scent of burning rubber in the air.

Window rolling down, the inspector stuck his arm out the window as he drove away, aiming a middle finger back in my direction. As if the situation were all *my* fault. I wasn't the thief here.

"I can't believe I told that ass about the downspout overflow problem," I muttered.

18

AFTER THE INSPECTOR'S VAN WAS OUT OF SIGHT, JASMINE STEPPED out from between two cars. She peered warily up and down our lane before walking fully into it.

"I almost changed right in the driver's seat," she told me as she walked up. "Not like *that* would have helped if an entire van smashed into the front of my car."

"Jasmine," Bolin blurted, dusting off his clothes.

I eyed the parking lot for signs of lingering vines but didn't see any. Had he done that with potions or bath bombs? With the one I'd witnessed close up, it had looked like he'd used sheer power to make it sprout.

"Hi, Bolin. Were you the one to stop the van?" Jasmine tilted her head and smiled at him. "I thought I saw... things."

"I, uhm." He looked helplessly at me.

Torn between wanting her to know he'd helped and his natural inclination to hide his power?

"He did stop the van," I said firmly. Jasmine already knew about his druidic tendencies. What was there to hide? "He's been developing his abilities and is turning into a strong ally."

I didn't mention the screaming over the slashed strap of the man purse. With luck, Jasmine had arrived *after* all that.

"Yes." Bolin nodded. "It's, uhm, good to see you." He brushed off his clothes again, though they appeared fine to me.

Jasmine looked down the lane to where her car had almost been flattened. "The help was well timed."

"Yes," Bolin said.

For a spelling-bee champion who knew a few bazillion words, he could get laconic at times.

"Bolin was wondering if you like non-alcoholic espresso martinis, Jasmine," I said.

"Oh? I've never had one. That sounds really interesting though."

"Would you like to come over sometime?" Bolin asked. "I can make you one."

I raised my eyebrows, wondering if he'd been looking up recipes during our battle.

"I..." Jasmine looked at me, as if I should advise her on who she should date. Or maybe she wondered if a *date* was what Bolin wanted. He wasn't the most direct about stating his interest in women.

I shrugged, feeling I'd done enough and that it was up to them to figure out if they were interested in each other. When she and I had discussed Bolin before, she'd been ambivalent. No, she'd compared him to her father. That was never a good sign.

But she looked toward the spot of her almost-collision again, then whispered to me, "He's *not* an omega."

"No," I murmured. "I think he has potential to be badass."

Bolin's eyebrows rose hopefully, though I didn't think he'd caught all that.

Jasmine smiled at Bolin. "I do like espresso-flavored things."

His heart melted into a puddle in the parking lot at his feet.

The sounds of gunfire coming from the apartment complex

next door made us all jump. Had the inspector stopped over there for some reason? I ran to the street and was in time to see a familiar armored SUV roar out of the parking lot with a wolf atop it. *Duncan.*

He crouched low to keep his balance as it sped into the street. Even in his bipedfuris form, where he had hands instead of paws, he'd struggled to stay on that vehicle. He couldn't even damage it as a wolf, could he?

When the window opened and one of Radomir's thugs leaned out with a rifle, I shouted for Duncan to look out. The guy rose up so that he could angle the gun toward his rooftop invader.

Even with the SUV racing away, Duncan managed to keep his balance enough to snap his jaws around the weapon before it fired. He flung it away. At the corner, the SUV made a hard turn, and Duncan flew off. He landed on his feet, but the vehicle sped away.

"I guess that's why he couldn't come right away to get the case," I said, relieved that Duncan didn't appear injured.

He glared in the direction the SUV had gone but must have decided he couldn't catch it. From that intersection, it was a quick drive to the nearest freeway entrance. Had Radomir or Abrams been inside? Waiting for a *report* from their building inspector?

"More like for the case to be delivered into their hands."

I wanted to check on it, but concern for Duncan overrode that desire, and I headed toward him. He was halfway to me when he swished his tail, then disappeared into a copse of trees and bushes. Had he left his clothes in there? Yes, he soon came out in human form, tugging his jacket on as he walked toward me. He glanced at his phone as he did so.

"Sorry." He waved it, my text message on the screen. "I think I was already changing when you sent this. That bloke didn't get the artifact, did he?"

"No. I stopped him and his werewolf buddy in time."

"Werewolf? I didn't sense one of our kind here, but as soon as I spotted that SUV, my focus was on it. Radomir was in the back. *Waiting.*"

"I knew this was all a ruse." I shook my head, disappointed that Duncan hadn't managed to catch Radomir. Had his weakened state worked against him? Though I wondered, I didn't ask, not wanting to make him feel worse than he probably already did.

"I'm sorry I didn't manage to capture him," Duncan said quietly, perhaps guessing at my thoughts.

"Don't worry about it." I was more disappointed on his behalf than with him. "We'll get another chance."

"I hope so." Duncan's conflicted expression suggested he didn't know how much time he had.

Concerned, I started to hug him, but Jasmine was waving to us. When she caught my eye, she pointed to her phone.

"Maybe that's our opportunity now." I touched Duncan's shoulder, then led the way back through the parking lot toward her.

"Is her father doing research for you again?" Duncan walked at my side.

"Yes. It's also possible that she and Bolin have agreed on an espresso-martini recipe and are excited about it."

Bolin, who'd retrieved his maligned man purse, didn't look that excited. Glum was the word to describe his expression as he considered the cut strap. I was surprised the small multitool blade had managed to sever it that quickly, but the inspector might have applied some of whatever type of power he possessed. I was lucky he hadn't managed to thwart the locks and get into my truck.

"I might need to get that repaired for Bolin," I said as we approached.

"That's a Stefano Ricci, isn't it?" Duncan asked. "It might cost a pretty penny."

"You think it's a lot more work to sew the strap of a luxury brand than a knockoff?"

"I think those who do the repairs know which clients they can charge more to than others." Duncan waved toward Bolin, the gesture including his expensive SUV.

"If I show up in my Goodwill clothes and my beat-up truck, they should give me a discount."

Duncan gazed thoughtfully at me. "I suppose that's possible. You could also show them your fangs. That can make craftsmen agreeable about offering deals."

"I'm not a brute."

"What should we do with the ladder you clubbed that man with, Luna?" Bolin asked as we walked up.

Duncan raised his eyebrows.

"He tried to club me first," I told him.

"Naturally."

"I'm *not* a brute."

Duncan smiled. "Certainly not."

Jasmine stepped close enough to show me her phone. "Dad found a newspaper article with photos of that glowy hand thing. It sold at an auction in this area a few years back."

"At what kind of auction does one buy magical artifacts?" Bolin asked.

"This was an art auction." Jasmine pointed at the heading.

"That thing didn't feel artsy as it was boring agony into my brain," I said.

"Dad did some digging and managed to find the name of the person who bought it. The *company* anyway." She showed me.

"TBL Luxury Perfumes and Potions." I recognized the umbrella company for Radomir's various businesses. "Looks like he's been collecting magical artifacts for years."

"There wasn't anything wolfish about that tool," Duncan said, "not that I noticed."

"Only that it was happy to thrust lances of pain-inducing power at a werewolf," I said.

"That describes more artifacts than you'd like."

"Throughout history, people have been afraid of powerful, shaggy beings," Bolin said.

"Unfair," Jasmine said. "They're not as scary as out-of-control vans."

"You think there should be more artifacts with the ability to zap those?" I asked.

"I do." She nodded firmly. "Anyway, Dad got the address that was associated with the company too. Apparently, the auction was online, and the buyer had the tool shipped afterward."

"Is it one of the places from the list your father put together before?" I leaned close to the phone to read it.

"No. I don't recognize it. Maybe we should check it out though."

"Wait." I held up a finger. "*I* recognize it."

But where had I seen it before? Jasmine was right that it wasn't on the earlier list of addresses her father had dredged up. I'd seen it… I flexed my fingers in the air, groping for the where and when. "Oh," I blurted and pulled out my own phone.

"Oh?" Jasmine peered at it.

I flipped through the recent photos, then found one I'd taken of a shipping label on a box in the mushroom farm.

"When I saw this, I figured it belonged to an alchemist client that Radomir's business was shipping mushrooms to." I showed them the screen.

"Maple Falls?" Duncan asked. "That's quite the happening little town."

"Yes, and that thug I tackled at the theater said he'd delivered my sword to a laboratory in that area." I tapped the address into my map app. Driving directions appeared, heading to a location well east of the gas station and grocery store that marked the center of town. "Do you want to check it out?"

Right after the words came out, I wished I hadn't asked. Duncan hadn't *fainted* anywhere, as I'd worried earlier, but with bags under his eyes and a slump to his usually straight posture, he looked exhausted. No, more than that. He looked like he was dying.

Tears threatened as I studied him.

"This auction was years ago?" Duncan was focused on the phone screen rather than on me getting teary-eyed. That was for the best. He wouldn't want me worrying about him. "It seems unlikely anyone is there now."

By the time he looked at my face, I'd blinked away the tears.

"The auction may have been years ago, but someone was shipping mushrooms there last week." I summed up my investigation at that property with Jasmine. We'd found Duncan *after* poking around there, so he hadn't seen the inside of that garage.

"Ah, interesting. It's a bit of a drive, but we don't have any better ideas about their location, so it might be worth checking out." Duncan looked wistfully in the direction the armored SUV had gone, doubtless wishing he'd managed to catch Radomir *here*. We could have been questioning him now instead of making plans to drive all over the Puget Sound area again.

"I can go. Maybe you can stay here and rest." I waved to his van, then looked at Jasmine and Bolin. Should I invite them along again? They'd been helpful in distracting the kidnappers at the cabin, but I worried about them being hurt. Especially Bolin. He wasn't a werewolf, and he wasn't a relative. What would I tell his parents if I got him killed?

"Rest?" Duncan asked. "It's the middle of the day."

"Yes, but you're..." I glanced at the others. "Looking peaked."

His eyebrows flew up, and he straightened. "Nothing a shot of caffeine won't fix. Let's visit your espresso maker. You have take-away mugs, don't you?"

"Several."

"That'll do." He nodded firmly.

Sadly, I doubted all the caffeine in the world would help him, but I nodded back. "Okay."

He was my biggest ally. Not taking him didn't seem right. Besides, if we found Radomir and Abrams, and they had a tool or artifact that could help him, he would need to be there for it to work.

"Do you want us to come, Aunt Luna?" Jasmine asked.

I bit my lip, considering them again. "Radomir and his building inspector might still be in the area. Would you stay here and keep an eye on things?"

"Things?" Bolin asked. "You mean the priceless artifact stuffed in your glovebox?"

"It wasn't stuffed. It was carefully placed inside. I even insulated it."

Bolin eyed the truck skeptically. Covering the case with a Kleenex possibly didn't count as insulation, but I hadn't crammed it in there.

"I could take it to my parents' house," he offered. "Dad has a safe, and it's a pretty secure spot. Their house also isn't due to have any *building inspections.*"

I hesitated. After Radomir had looked up my family and known all about Austin's trip home for the holidays, I assumed he also knew about my intern and his parents. Radomir probably had their address as well as that of Bolin's home. Still, leaving it in my apartment wouldn't be a good idea either, not after the supposed inspector had confirmed it was in the area.

"Maybe I'll take it with me," I said.

Bolin shrugged. "Suit yourself."

"And possibly deliver it into Radomir's hands?" Duncan asked.

"I doubt he's going to be up there when we get there." I *hoped* he would be, but that seemed a lot to ask. The guy was more nomadic than a homeless man living out of a shopping cart.

"We could guard it while making espresso-martini mocktails." Jasmine smiled at Bolin again.

He straightened. "Yes, we could. We wouldn't even be drunk."

"Sugar high, maybe," I murmured, watching as Jasmine clasped Bolin's hand. More to facilitate a potential budding relationship than to secure the artifact, I said, "Okay, go ahead. Keep an eye on it for me. I'll bring you a souvenir back from Maple Falls."

"We were just up there," Jasmine said. "I got a splinter in my tail in that cabin."

"I'll bring you a *better* souvenir," I assured her.

"Just get your sword back," Jasmine said. "And fix Duncan. He looks…"

"Peaked," I said.

"Yeah." Jasmine shrugged. "Sorry, Duncan."

"No worries," he said. "It'll play into our plan."

"Our plan?" I asked.

"I'm still ready and willing to faint on your enemies while you take them from behind."

"With a plan like that, how can we lose?"

19

Duncan and I headed north in his van, to-go cups of Americanos in the drink holders. He'd intended to drive, but, after witnessing him pass out once that day, I'd talked him out of it by saying I knew the area where we were going better than he, so it would be best for me to take the wheel. He'd given me a knowing look but allowed it and now sat in the passenger seat, his knees scrunched to his chest, the way I usually had to ride due to all the junk in the foot space.

Between us rested bags that we'd packed. I didn't know what his held, but I'd tucked the potions and druid bath bombs I'd collected these past weeks into mine. Also chocolate. One had to be well-provisioned for an adventure, after all.

"Are you sure those two will assiduously guard the artifact?" he asked as we navigated highway traffic on the way north. We'd left Bolin and Jasmine climbing into the G-Wagon as we departed. "They looked like they were having romantic inklings."

"He did save her life, or at least leap nobly to her defense and keep her car from being smashed to pieces."

"I've leaped to your defense a number of times, and it's yet to send you into my arms with smooches on your lips."

"I'm old, divorced, and jaded. It takes more to prompt smooch desires in me."

"You're not *old*, my lady. You're strong, vibrant, and delightful."

"Words like that might make my lips twitch in your direction."

"I do get excited by the prospect of twitching lips."

"In your current condition, I'm not sure we should get you excited."

"If there's to be no more *excitement* in my life, I might as well die now."

"If Radomir and Abrams are at that address when we arrive, things could get exciting."

"Probably not in the lip-twitching sort of way though." Duncan sighed. "Unless going into battle with vile nemeses rouses you more than I believe."

"*Surviving* such battles and lifting curses can get me pretty revved up."

"Ah." He rested his hand over his heart. "A reason to live."

"To live and kick some ass."

"Do you think doing so would prove my worth to the medallion?" His hand drifted to the wolf head hanging from his neck. "Ass kicking traditionally *is* how the alpha position is taken."

"I don't know what's in the minds—do medallions have minds?—of these artifacts. Too bad that one wasn't around when we were thumping my cousins. That should have proven your worth."

"*You* were the one to defeat the nefarious Augustus," Duncan pointed out.

"Maybe, but I wouldn't have if you hadn't been hurling explosives about."

"Maybe I'm supposed to defeat your current alpha," he mused.

"Lorenzo? Duncan, you can't kick the ass of the old guy looking after my sick mother."

"No? I may be at an impasse as far as proving goes then." He lowered his hand.

"Don't worry about the medallion. We're going to force Abrams to lift the curse." I nodded firmly at him and didn't mention my doubts about the address on the GPS. Our enemies had so *many* addresses that it would be sheer luck if we stumbled across them there. But maybe if the glowing mushrooms were delivered to that destination, it meant it was another potion factory. The kind of place where magical substances were made and where help for Duncan might be found? I hadn't heard anything from Rue about discoveries she'd made along that line, but Abrams and Radomir's operation was a lot larger.

"If only I could prove myself by finding a great treasure in the depths of a mysterious and hard-to-access body of water." Duncan sighed fondly at a magnet nestled on the pile of junk in the seat well.

"Are you going to obsess about this the whole way up there?"

"Maybe. It's not that long of a drive, is it?" He waved at the GPS map offering directions and a time estimate to our destination. "We'll be there before dark. I need something to occupy my thoughts until then."

"We could stop for an early dinner along the way." I didn't know if it would matter if we visited this place during daylight hours or at night. It might be easier to sneak in under the shroud of darkness, but who knew if it would even be worth sneaking in*to*? Scoping it out first seemed wise.

"Are you asking if I'd like to join you for a restaurant meal? We haven't done that since our first date."

"That hardly counted as a date. You fished a rusty fork out of the lake, and we had to battle mongrel dogs and wolves on a dock."

"My *lady*, what *else* would you want to do with a handsome gentleman? The teriyaki chicken skewers weren't without appeal, but they were made much tastier by the hunger we worked up beforehand."

"By battling wolves and rusty forks."

"Precisely. You were at my side for both. It was wondrous." He gazed over at me.

"I'm not sure whether to think you're odd or to be pleased that you enjoy having my company for such endeavors."

"*Both* should delight you, I would think."

We chatted amiably until we'd turned off the highway and were drawing closer to Maple Falls and our destination. Now and then, nerves intruded as I let myself think about what would happen if we didn't find a solution for Duncan, but I mostly managed to distract myself. His flirting, if that was what one would call it, helped. Maybe he was doing it intentionally, knowing I was worried. It seemed like I should be the one trying to distract him. Maybe we managed a bit of both.

Our banter had more lapses as we passed through town. Despite my earlier suggestion, we didn't stop for dinner. I didn't want to dillydally. After everything that had happened lately, being away from Sylvan Serenity made me uneasy. Radomir might even now be rounding up thugs to more forcibly search my apartment, thugs who could endanger the tenants. After all the violence on the premises, I was surprised more people hadn't moved out.

The GPS led us up a winding road that climbed into the hills. Fortunately, it was paved, and, now and then, we spotted residences through the trees to either side. With twilight descending, a couple of the homes had lights on. Judging by the number that didn't, this was another second-home area, probably sparsely populated by full-time residents.

Since we'd last been through Maple Falls, the snow on the ground had melted, but the white blanket covering Mount Baker was visible at various points as the van climbed in elevation. To our left, there was a cluster of mailboxes, followed by a lit gate with a sign proclaiming the name of a community and that it offered kayaking, fishing, and hiking, as well as resort amenities.

"Guess that's not our destination." I nodded to the map, the GPS wanting us to continue for another mile.

"It didn't look like the type of locale where one would set up a potion factory."

"You don't think Abrams likes to take breaks from mixing magical ingredients to hop in his kayak?"

"I believe he's reached the age where kayak-hopping may be contraindicated."

"But evil-overlord, take-over-the-world activities are fine."

"Oh, you can engage in those at *any* age." Duncan waved airily as we continued on, the headlights of the van the only illumination now.

"You'd think a certain amount of youthful ambition and vigor would be required."

"For those who crave leaving a legacy, ambition never goes away. We don't know, however, that taking over the *world* is their goal. They never confided in me."

"Whatever they're angling for with the werewolf artifacts, I doubt it's anything wholesome."

"No."

We bumped off the pavement and onto gravel. Did delivery vans truly take mushrooms all the way back here? If there were any more houses along the route, I couldn't make them out in the twilight gloom.

To the right, the trees we'd been driving through thinned and then disappeared altogether as the view opened up, revealing a steep cliff dropping sharply away. Only the most modest of low guard rails blocked a car from going over. On the other side of the road, an equally daunting vertical rock face rose up toward mountain-goat territory. Normally, heights didn't bother me, but my palms grew damp as I imagined another car coming from the other direction. Would there be room for it to pass us on the increasingly narrow road?

"There's no way a FedEx truck comes up this," I stated.

"Maybe deliveries are dropped off back at the cluster of mailboxes we passed."

"Yeah." I glanced at the map. We'd reached the end of the line. In fact, it looked like we had missed a turn. "Crap."

"I didn't see any driveways or side roads we could have taken," Duncan said.

"The GPS might have been leading us astray all along." With few options, I continued on. "I'll turn around as soon as I can."

Duncan peered out the side window at the deep descent. "There's a stream down there."

"I'm not stopping so you can magnet fish."

He laughed. "I don't believe we would find much in such a remote locale."

"You'd have to go back downstream to where the kayaking happens."

"Most assuredly."

I spotted a turnout ahead and let out a relieved breath. Though I didn't like that it was on the side of the road with the drop-off, it was wide enough that we could use it to point the van back in the other direction.

"I'm turning around there," I said. "We can go back and check the addresses on the mailboxes. See if we're even in the right spot."

As I pulled onto the turnout, a distant light came into view around a bend farther up the road. It was halfway up the side of a treed slope.

"You've got to be kidding me," I said.

Duncan had noticed it too. "That's a much more likely location for someone to live while plotting to take over the world."

"No resort amenities there, I'll bet."

"Continue on?" Duncan extended his hand toward the road.

I grimaced at the windshield. It looked like the road moved away from the cliff to climb toward that slope, but it took me a moment before I could convince myself to continue along it. Possibly because I remembered being chased away from the mushroom farm by Radomir's thugs in his armored tank. No cliffs had been involved that night, but the experience had been harrowing.

"Do you want me to drive the rest of the way?" Duncan must have noticed my expression—or maybe my white-knuckled grip on the wheel.

"This is the *last* place I would want my driver to faint."

"Understandable. I'll simply sit over here and beam moral support at you."

"Thanks."

We continued on. Fortunately, after the bend, the road meandered away from the cliff. It turned to dirt as it switch-backed up the side of the slope toward the single light that we could intermittently see through the trees. I didn't try to hide the relieved dabbing of sweat from my forehead when the forest once again rose on either side of us.

Ahead, a sturdy iron gate blocked the road, a brick wall with two rows of barbed wire on top stretching to either side.

"Final destination," I murmured while considering a gravel parking area outside the gate. Near it, a keypad mounted on a post glowed softly. "For those who know the code."

"Or fancy hopping over some barbed wire," Duncan said.

"That's a tall fence to *hop*."

The light we'd seen was inside the fenced compound, mounted on a cement wall visible beyond the gate.

"For those with our athletic aptitude," Duncan said, "it shouldn't be too difficult."

I looked at him, and he raised a finger.

"Don't mention fainting again," he said. "It's not going to happen."

"That's good because if you passed out with one leg over barbed wire, you might maim something important."

"I'm glad you deem my body parts important, even the ones you haven't had an opportunity to fully admire yet."

"I've seen you naked a bunch of times." I parked by the gate.

"That's not the same as taking your time to lovingly admire something. *Some* body parts need a close examination, ideally with an accompanying tactile experience."

"For someone with a dire medical condition, you've had intimacy on your mind a lot." After turning off the van, I handed him the keys.

"I've been lamenting that we never got a chance to engage in said intimacy."

"I've lamented that too," I admitted, smiling sadly at him.

"I suppose this wouldn't be the place."

"I doubt you can even..." I waved vaguely toward his lap. "In your condition."

"Really, Luna. You'd be amazed at what I can do in *any* condition." Despite the words, he opened the door and stepped out. Maybe, even if he were able, he agreed that the driveway in front of the enemy's compound wasn't the appropriate place for intimate activities.

I joined him outside to peek through the gate.

Patches of snow dotted the ground, pine cones scattered in between, and a large cement-and-steel rectangle of a building rose up in the middle. It had no ground-floor windows, but rows of small glass squares lined what was likely the second story. Those windows hadn't been designed to let one admire the mountain views. Rather, they were small enough to keep anyone from climbing through them. On one end of the building, a solid ground-floor door was made from metal with another keypad on the wall beside it. From our spot, we couldn't see the other end.

Once before, Duncan had ripped a metal door off its hinges, but would he have the strength for that now?

A few floral scents wafted through the chill air, noticeable above the forest smells of pine, Douglas fir, and moss. There were other scents as well, but I struggled to identify them. Chemicals? Ingredients for potions? Who knew?

"It doesn't look like anyone is home." Duncan waved toward the grounds at the lack of automobiles visible. The way the building was built into the slope made it unlikely that any were parked behind it.

"You may not get any opportunities to prove yourself."

"Alas."

"Unless the medallion would be impressed by you flexing your great muscles and yanking that door open."

"I have to imagine it would be, but I brought some grenades along, should my great muscles prove insufficient to the task."

"Had time to shop at the military-surplus store, did you?"

"I believe we've both appreciated having a stockpile of explosives lately."

"Is it a sign that my life has become strange that I'm quick to nod yes to that?"

"*Very* strange." Duncan opened the sliding door, climbed into his van, and grabbed a few items, tucking them into his pack.

I grabbed my own bag, then gripped the wrought-iron bars of the gate and tried to extend my senses toward the building, to tell if any magical items lay within. Yes, I *did* sense magic but couldn't tell if it was powerful enough to suggest artifacts. More likely, the building held numerous glowing mushrooms and other paranormal potion ingredients. Though I did get a sense of more magic underground. In a basement? The walls and ground were insulating and made it hard to tell what kind of magic might be down there.

Duncan grunted as he slung the pack over his shoulders, then gripped the bars and climbed the gate. Like the wall, it had barbed-wire at the top, but he managed to navigate over it without scraping himself to pieces—or fainting.

"Not going to rip anything off the hinges tonight?" I waved toward the side of the gate, then grabbed the bars to see if I could emulate his climb. There weren't any decorative curlicues that would have made ideal footholds, but a horizontal metal bar in the middle helped.

"There might be a security system." Duncan hopped down on the inside of the gate. "If so, ripping doors and gates asunder is the kind of thing that sets alarms off."

"Have you experienced that in your various adventures?"

"I might have, yes." Duncan pointed out a couple of security cameras mounted on the cement walls as I climbed down beside him. "It's human nature for people to want to protect their valuables."

"Have you gotten caught before trying to get into a secured compound?"

"Usually, the treasures I hunt are in a lost-at-sea or buried-underground state and rarely secured, but I might have had to skedaddle at a rapid pace a few times to avoid Dobermans, Rottweilers, and brutes with tasers."

"Those sound like harrowing experiences," I said, though a werewolf shouldn't have trouble handling any of those foes.

"A little harrowing, a little exhilarating."

"Apparently, nothing untoward enough happened to change your life, or you wouldn't be fishing for coins in private koi ponds."

"*Those* are rarely surrounded by cameras and alarm systems."

"Strange that people don't value their fish more."

One of the security cameras on the walls swiveled on its mount to face us. Though I doubted anyone was on the premises, I wouldn't be surprised if those were transmitting back to one of Radomir's paid people. We would have to do our snooping swiftly, before someone arrived to stop us—at gunpoint.

Perhaps thinking the same, Duncan trotted for the door we'd observed. It was locked, and 1-2-3-4 did not open the keypad.

He jogged around the building to check for other entrances. I eyed the second-story windows. From below, they were larger than I'd thought. I *might* be able to squeeze through one. Duncan, with his broader shoulders, was iffier. Not that I saw an easy way up to and through them from the outside regardless. They were flush with the flat and unadorned cement walls.

"There's another man door and a large roll-up garage door on that side of the building," Duncan said when he returned. "But they're locked and very sturdy. There aren't any lower-level windows, and the walls are smooth, not conducive to climbing."

He gripped the door handle in front of me, planted a foot on the wall, and tested it by pulling. It didn't budge.

"I've lost a wee bit of my strength," he admitted reluctantly, releasing the handle. "Or it might be that this door is a little sturdier than the one at the other compound."

"For the sake of your ego, I'll say that it's *clearly* much thicker and better made."

"You're a good woman." Duncan shrugged off his pack and pulled out a grenade.

"Are we giving up on the plan not to trigger the security system and going forward with ripping things asunder?"

"I've caught the cameras tracking me. I believe someone already knows we're here." Duncan waved for me to back away, armed and set the grenade against the door, then ran to join me.

We ducked behind a well house a second before it blew, the explosion thunderous as it echoed across the mountainside. I imagined someone at the resort community pausing in putting away their kayak for the day to look curiously in this direction.

"I hope we have the right address," I said when the noise of the explosion faded.

"We do." Duncan peered toward the entrance.

"The GPS was less certain."

"The GPS couldn't sense magical potion ingredients inside." Duncan cocked his head as the smoke cleared, revealing the door blown open. Surprisingly, the wall around it hadn't been damaged. That had to be made from something sturdier than the cement it looked like. "And not *only* ingredients, I think. I can pick up more magic now that there's a hole in the wall. *Stronger* magic. Lots of it. It's below ground, I believe."

"I'm ready." I flexed my fingers, surprising myself by again wishing I had the sword. Maybe I just wanted something with which to defend myself. But, with night deepening, I trusted I could easily turn into a wolf inside, if need be.

"Something a man always enjoys hearing from a lady." Duncan saluted me, then led the way toward the entrance, the smoke mostly cleared, though enough lingered to make my nostrils itch.

"There wasn't this much innuendo when I went on a mission with Bolin and my niece." I followed him to the doorway.

"Oh? Was it a superior experience?"

"Not really. I had to listen to violin rap music."

"My flirty wit must be a vast improvement."

"You think so?"

"I do," he said with confidence.

We stepped into a wide dark corridor, the interior walls and floor made from the same gray cement—or whatever it was—as the exterior. Only the ceiling was made from a lesser material, something flat and white with a metallic sheen. Few doors occupied the flat walls, and no lights came on as we entered. There weren't switches anywhere in sight, though modern recessed lamps lined the ceiling. If one could figure out how to turn them on.

If not for the exterior light, I might have believed the power was out. There were also a couple of green glowing circles set into the wall halfway down the hallway. Odd.

A lot of faint *tink, tink, tink* sounds came from the distance. Almost like water dripping but more mechanical in nature.

"This looks more modern than most of their other hideouts," Duncan observed.

"I take it Radomir and Abrams never summoned you to this place?" I tapped on the flashlight app on my phone. Even with keener than typical night vision, it was hard to see everything.

Ah, was that an *elevator* by those green circles? Those had to be the up-down buttons.

"They did not. I would say it's unlikely they use the facility, but I smell Abrams's scent here. Not only has he visited often, but he's visited recently. I—"

A loud clang sounded behind us. I jumped and spun, landing in a ready stance, my skin pricking in alarm, the wolf almost tempted out by the noise.

A gate of thick steel bars had descended to block the doorway.

"I... didn't expect that after we blew our way in," Duncan said.

"Security is better here than you'd expect in such a remote facility."

"Better than in a koi pond."

"No doubt."

Duncan jogged to the gate, gripped the bars, and attempted to lift them. They didn't budge. He crouched to give it a more serious try. Given his strength, however diminished by the curse, I expected him to be able to heft open the gate, but the bars still didn't budge.

Hell. We were trapped.

20

"WE MIGHT WANT TO EXPEDITE OUR SNOOPING," I SAID TO STOP
Duncan from straining at the bars.

Earlier, I'd been joking about him fainting—mostly—but
when he slumped against the wall, weary from his exertion, I
worried it was a real possibility.

He noticed my concerned expression and straightened, then
nodded firmly. "Right. We'll likely have company soon."

"Maybe they'll know how to open the gate."

"One would hope. Though I do have more grenades." Duncan
opened a pocket on his pack, pulled out two, and handed one to
me. "They're in limited supply though, so let's make sure we don't
need them for something else before hurling them at those bars.
Especially since we're *inside* the building now."

"Okay." I didn't see evidence that the first explosion had
damaged the structure, but it might be different if we detonated
one from within the building.

Duncan cocked his head. "Is it my imagination, or are the
magical items we've been sensing *moving*?"

He pointed at the floor.

"I get that feeling too." I thought of the magical bats that had dive-bombed me in a cave not that long ago.

We walked down the hallway, pausing at the infrequent doors. Like the one we'd blown up, they were made from metal, all shut and locked.

As Duncan had pointed out, I sensed magic in what had to be a basement or crawlspace underneath us. More than ingredients for potions. Something moving. Something alive?

Before we reached the elevator, a *bing* sounded. One of the green circular lights brightened.

"Uhm." I pointed my flashlight in that direction, picking out a stairwell next to the elevator. From down the hallway, it was hard to tell, but it looked to offer up and down options. "We may want to—"

Run up the stairs to avoid being spotted, I'd intended to say. But the elevator doors opened first.

I crouched, tensing. Duncan also crouched, his fingers curling, and growled. Could he summon the bipedfuris in his weakened state?

Rapid *tinks* sounded as something skittered out of the elevator. A giant metal... bug?

The mechanical construct was beetle-shaped, its carapace more than a foot wide. Including its eight legs, it rose equally tall. It lacked a distinct head, but when it rotated toward us, two glowing red eyes pointed in our direction, and something like a jaw lowered to show a round orifice. One might call it a mouth, but it didn't have teeth or appear flexible.

Without moving its legs, its body rotated left and right, though those red eyes never shifted their focus from us. The jaw opened and closed a couple of times, and a faint cloud of vapor wafted from its orifice, reminding me of one's breath on a cold morning. It hazed the air in front of the glowing eyes, but only for a moment before dissipating. Then the mechanical creature skittered back into the elevator, and the doors closed.

"Huh," Duncan said.

"Nothing you've seen before in any of their lairs?"

"It is not, but I did sense that it was magical."

"Yeah. If it's what we're sensing in the basement, there are a lot more of them."

The *tinks* I'd been hearing continued on, drifting up from the stairs. The sounds of mechanical beetle legs on a hard floor? I imagined a horde of those bugs down there.

"Why don't we see what's upstairs first?" I suggested.

"I'm amenable to that. Though the garage doors on the far side of the building would be that way, if we want to see if we can escape through one of them." Duncan pointed toward a metal door at the end of the hall.

"We haven't accomplished our mission yet. Besides, the garage doors probably have bars over them now too."

"A distinct possibility."

I headed for the stairs, hoping the upper level held offices filled with filing cabinets of information, or something else useful. Such as a collection of potions that could lift curses...

As we reached the stairs, the door at the end of the hall opened, seemingly of its own accord. I expected a squad of Radomir's potion-enhanced thugs to charge through it with guns. Instead, another large metal bug *tinked* out, red eyes glowing. It was identical to the first one.

The construct looked at us for a long moment, then skittered back out of sight. I had a glimpse of a dark cavernous room that might have been the garage before the door thudded shut.

More *tinks* sounded behind us, from the direction we'd come. A side door along the hallway had opened, one that we'd tried and had been locked. One of the bug robots skittered into view. It stopped in front of the bars of the gate that had descended, then turned to face us, as if it were a guard dog prepared to defend that exit.

If we needed to depart that way, I would happily throw one of the grenades at it as well as the gate.

"Upstairs we go." Duncan glanced uneasily at the creature watching us, then took the lead.

"You're not intimidated by those little bugs, are you? You tore a robot dog to literal pieces not long ago."

"I did. There was only one of it, though, and an intriguing water-filled hole behind it to explore."

"The things you find intriguing are a little odd."

"I find *you* intriguing." He smiled over his shoulder at me.

"Yeah, and my kids would be the first to tell you that's odd." I thought of Austin's letter and what he might have discussed with Cameron but pushed the musings away. This wasn't the time to be distracted.

As we climbed the cement steps, I wondered if the bugs were capable of clambering up them. Maybe they always took the elevator. How they pushed the buttons from the floor, I couldn't guess. Magic? Access to a wireless network? Who knew?

"No bugs up here," Duncan said as we stepped into a hallway similar to the one below, though small square windows marked each end instead of doors.

Bars had come down over those windows, bars that hadn't been in place when I'd looked at them from outside.

I eyed my single grenade, hoping it would be as easy to leave when we were done as Duncan believed. After watching the cameras track us, I had little doubt that someone besides the guard bugs knew we were here and was probably on the way.

We looked through an open door into what reminded me of a break room in an office building. It had a fridge and cabinets but wasn't a full kitchen.

"I was expecting a potion-making factory, like the other place," I said, heading to the next room.

"Maybe that's done in the basement."

Which I wasn't eager to explore if it was full of mechanical guard bugs. But the other rooms we checked upstairs weren't any more promising, most holding desks or bedroom furniture. None of the drawers had anything in them, nor did I find my sword propped in the corner anywhere. Not that I'd expected that. I didn't sense any magic on this floor.

We didn't find any stairs leading up to the roof and debated our options when we returned to the elevator.

"Can you tell if any of the magic we can sense down there belongs to tools or artifacts?" I pointed at the floor. "Something *important*?"

I doubted the bugs could lift Duncan's curse.

"It might," he said. "There's enough magic that it's hard to identify individual signatures. My senses suggest there are a lot of those bugs down there."

"Mine too, unfortunately."

Duncan pressed one of the elevator buttons. When the doors opened, I braced myself, expecting the bug we'd seen earlier to walk out. But the elevator car was empty.

We stepped in, and Duncan held his finger over the two options. Level 1 or Basement. He looked at me.

We hadn't checked all the rooms on the first floor, but my gut told me we wouldn't find anything of interest on that level. We also might not have much time before the security squad arrived.

"Let's find out what the guard bugs are guarding." I held up the grenade to show him I was ready for trouble.

"Agreed, but don't throw that unless you really need to, especially not in the basement."

"Afraid the entire building would come down on us?"

"That *is* a possibility." Duncan pressed the basement button.

As soon as the doors opened, dozens and dozens of *tinks* reached our ears, and numerous sets of glowing red eyes turned toward us. It had been dark upstairs, but down here, it was pitch-black, save for those eyes. The air smelled both floral and musty with a hint of decay. I remembered the odor of the mushroom farm and suspected the ingredients that had been mailed to this address were stored down here.

Duncan turned on his phone's flashlight app and swung the beam over the red eyes. In the cavernous space, it shined on metal vats, wood and plastic crates, and white barrels that held chemicals or other liquids. A couple of those barrels had skull-and-crossbones stickers on the side. One claimed its contents were radioactive.

"Another reason not to throw a grenade down here," I said.

The flashlight beam also reflected on the metallic carapaces of dozens and dozens of metal bugs, all rotated to face us. A couple of them puffed out soft breaths of vapor, the same as the one above. Well, not *breaths*, I supposed. They wouldn't have lungs and be breathing; at least, I couldn't imagine that. But guessing what those little clouds might be made me uneasy. With so many other odors in the area, I couldn't tell what the vapor smelled like or guess what it was.

Something toxic?

"I don't see a light switch," Duncan said.

"Maybe the lights are voice-activated, and you have to know a secret word to turn them on."

"Could be." Duncan pointed toward a door behind the bugs, one of a couple off the cavernous room. "Think they'll let us go that way?"

"We're powerful and mighty werewolves. How would they stop us?" Even as I asked the question, I eyed another puff of vapor in front of the eyes of a nearby bug. For a few seconds, I thought I caught a sweet odor that didn't fit in with the pervasive floral, mushroom, and chemical scents.

"Maybe we should have brought your SCUBA equipment, so we wouldn't have had to breathe the air in here," I said.

"I did notice they're emitting... something." Duncan sniffed. "Abrams's scent is down here, even stronger than above."

I struggled to pick out the odor of a human above everything else but couldn't and took his word for it. Not only did he have keener senses than I did, but he knew Abrams well.

Duncan took a few steps, trying to skirt the main horde of bugs —or would it be a *swarm*?—to reach the door he'd indicated. Why he wanted to enter that one over the others, I didn't know, but I *could* sense magic behind it.

The also-magical bugs shifted to block him.

He stopped. "Hm."

"What do you think happens if you step on one?" I walked around the core of the mass. Maybe one of us could reach that door while the bugs were focused on the other.

"They look sturdy. It might take you for a ride." Duncan walked around the other side of the mass, angling for the door.

A hint of whirring joined the *tinks* as the creatures shifted about. Several moved to block the door before Duncan reached it. They formed a distinct barrier, shifting together when he tried to step around them. A couple opened and closed their orifices, and that tinge of sweetness grew stronger.

The hair on the back of my neck rose, and I caught myself backing away. My instincts told me we didn't want to inhale a lot of that vapor.

"They've got some intelligence about them, don't they?" Duncan paused his advance again. He sounded like he'd reached the same conclusion about the vapor and was trying not to breathe deeply.

"For chunks of metal without heads, yeah."

They hadn't attacked yet, but the blood flowing through my veins was tingling as heat flushed my skin. My magic promised the wolf was available if I wanted to change.

Did I? In my lupine form, I couldn't open doors, and the thought of gnashing down on metal carapaces held no appeal.

I rubbed my thumb over the grenade in my hand, thinking that might be the more appropriate weapon here. But Duncan's warning came to mind, and I eyed the barrels as well as the ceiling. The visible metal support beams appeared sturdy, but there was a lot of weight in the cement walls on the floors above.

Duncan backed away from the swarm, circled a few barrels and vats, and walked toward another door. Looking over his shoulder, he watched the metal bugs. When he approached the door, they didn't move.

"Good try." I assumed he'd thought he might lure them away so I could get into the first door.

"There might not be anything important in this one." It wasn't locked, and Duncan opened it to peek in. "It's a supply closet larger than my whole van."

"Your *van* isn't that large."

"It's a reasonably sized space." He stepped into the closet and shined his light on shelves filled with canned and dehydrated food.

"You can't tell me you don't long for more room for your treasure-hunting equipment."

"Well *everyone* longs for more room for that. Creamed corn? These look more like supplies for a fall-out shelter than ingredients for magical recipes."

"You don't think Rue puts that in her wart-infliction potion?"

"She doesn't have any corn hanging in twists from her ceiling." Again eyeing the bugs, Duncan walked to another door.

This time, a few moved, but they didn't rush to block it. When Duncan opened it, out floated strong scents of dried herbs, flowers, and was that a hint of moss? He stood in the doorway, looking upon tables and counters.

"A laboratory?" he mused. "Abrams's scent is even stronger in here."

"You think it's where he does his... what work is it exactly that he does? Besides cloning old-world werewolves?"

"Research. Or so he always told me." Duncan walked inside.

A couple of bugs skittered after him.

"You're being followed," I warned him as he investigated the laboratory.

"I see that." He disappeared from view. Thumps and clanks drifted out as he opened what sounded like metal drawers and cabinets.

The bugs trailed him around the room. Why did I have a feeling they had cameras and the ability to record?

With several of the swarm facing the laboratory, seemingly distracted by Duncan, I tried to get to the first door.

But the ones that had remained to guard it rotated toward me. The red eyes of one flared, and its orifice opened. A denser cloud of vapor than I'd yet seen wafted out.

I backed away, the sweet scent strong in the air. Too bad there weren't windows down here that one could open.

A numbness crept up from the ends of my fingers and into my arms. And did my eyelids feel heavy? Or was that my imagination? That vapor could be something that would knock us out.

"There are some magical tools in here," Duncan called.

"Any swords?"

"Not that I've seen. It might not be here."

"That would be annoying. I didn't come all the way up here just to see the sights. The bizarre multi-legged, robot-bug sights."

More *tinks* sounded as they shuffled around.

"I thought you came to find a way to lift my curse," Duncan said.

"I did. Have you found it yet?" I eyed the blocked door. Though there were probably some artifacts in the laboratory, the greatest concentration of magic that I sensed came from beyond *this* door. Something back there even felt familiar, though I couldn't identify the aura with any certainty. Still, the memory of being in Radomir and Abrams's office with numerous artifacts lined up on the desk came to me.

"I haven't." Duncan stepped into view in the doorway. "These magical needle-nosed pliers are somewhat intriguing though." He held up the tool, the tips glowing a slight blue.

"I could use a new pair," I said, "but I suppose we should only take what's been taken from us."

"Your tenants might be alarmed if you came to repair their faucets with glowing tools."

"That is true. Though the ghost hunters might be delighted."

Duncan walked toward the back of the swarm, again eyeing the one door we'd been denied access to. He rubbed the tips of his fingers together.

"Are they numb?" I asked.

He lowered his hand. "Tingling, yes."

"I think it's that gas or vapor or whatever you'd call it. I don't advise breathing it."

"I think you're right." Duncan withdrew a grenade. "I'm aching to see what's in that room."

"You advised me against hurling explosives in a basement."

"I did, didn't I?"

"If the bugs have reservoirs of that gas in their bellies, blowing *them* up might not be a good idea either."

"That's a good point. Maybe I can get them to chase me, and you can check out that room."

"They're not dogs, and you don't have a raw steak in your back pocket."

"No, but, oh!" Duncan snapped his fingers and jogged back into the laboratory.

Soon, the roar of a jet engine came from within, and I raised my eyebrows.

"Ventilation fan," he called.

"You think it's powerful enough to suck vapors all the way from in here?"

"We'll punt the bugs in there if we have to. I *know* there's something worth seeing in that other room." Jaw firm, he reappeared and pointed his chin at the door that had been denied to us, then strode toward it.

Once more, the bugs shifted about, clumping together to block his path. He picked one up, looking like he intended to hurl it into the laboratory, but it flashed white, and he dropped it.

"Bloody hell. They're electrified."

Numerous orifices opened, and a great puff of vapor clouded the air. Duncan and I were the ones to jog into the laboratory, closing the door behind us. We huddled in front of the noisy industrial fan he'd turned on. The air soon smelled clearer.

"There aren't any protective suits in here, are there?" I asked.

"Something like your oven mitt but full body?"

I snorted, reminded of all the times I'd used the mitt to pick up the wolf case. "Something more effective than that I'd hope. Like a hazmat suit."

"I haven't seen any yet." Duncan poked into closets and looked in a refrigerator filled with racks of vials with different colored liquids in them.

A couple of the metal bugs clinked around outside the laboratory.

"Obnoxious things." I looked at the time on my phone, pondering how long it might take for Radomir to send hordes of his thugs up here to check on a breach in the security.

"Quite." Duncan leaned his hands against a flat section of wall without any cabinets or counters blocking it. It appeared to be made from metal, similar to the door. Sturdy metal. "The room the bugs are denying us access to should be on the other side of this wall."

"Did you bring a blowtorch?"

"I was hoping *you* did."

"I only brought important supplies." I delved into my pocket and held up an unopened bar of dark chocolate laced with sea salt and dried huckleberries.

"That *is* important, but it sadly won't get us through such a sturdy wall." Duncan thumped the side of his fist on it. It didn't sound like it was as thick and solid as the exterior walls of the building, but the metal wouldn't be easily destroyed.

"Could a bipedfuris rip through it?"

"Maybe, but..." Duncan looked grimly at me.

"What?"

"I've tried to change a couple of times now, thinking I might be able to destroy those beasties out there faster than they could gas us."

"And?"

"The power is eluding me. I'm... stuck as a man."

21

"I'M SURE THERE'S PLENTY YOU CAN DO AS A MAN," I SAID TO Duncan's dejected head shake.

"Not right now, unfortunately." He slumped against the wall but only for a second before he returned to searching cabinets and drawers. "There are answers in that room over there, Luna. I'm sure of it."

I removed my bag and poked into it, hoping I'd packed something that might prove useful. I had one of Bolin's Orbs of Entanglement spheres. Might I throw that in a spot that would cause most of the bugs to stick to it? I lifted the sphere, on the verge of suggesting that, when I remembered the sample that Rue had given me the last time I'd ordered potions from her.

"Do you think a delightfully versatile blue-spider acid might go through that wall?" Those had been her descriptors when she'd given the vial to me. I fished through my belongings until I found it.

"I've never heard of that before, but the word *acid* sounds promising in this context." Duncan walked over to consider the wall again. "Applying it to a vertical surface would be challenging. I don't suppose it came with an applicator brush?"

"It's not a tube of eye shadow." I offered the vial to him in case he wanted to try it. "There have to be droppers or something in a laboratory though, right?"

Ticks at the door made me jump. Were those bugs *knocking*?

"Don't answer that." Duncan jogged toward one of the drawers he'd investigated.

"You think? It's not like it's going to be Dominos."

"Indeed." Duncan pulled out a kit with glass droppers. "You'd have to tip quite profusely to entice a delivery driver up here, I believe."

"*Very* profusely."

Duncan took the vial from me, carefully removed the lid, and walked to the wall. He started to slip the dropper into the vial but paused.

More *ticks* came from the door. Maybe the bugs weren't knocking as much as trying to find a way in. Since they could use the elevator, I wouldn't put it past them to figure out a door.

"Glass is impervious to most acids but not hydrofluoric acid," Duncan said. "Do you know what all is in blue-spider liquid?"

"Besides blue spiders? I haven't a clue. Just smear some on there, and let's see if it does anything."

Even if the stuff could eat through cement and metal, it was hard to imagine such a small amount of liquid being sufficient to make a hole big enough to crawl through. I assumed that was what Duncan had in mind. Still, the liquid in the vial *was* magical. Maybe it would surprise me.

"As my lady commands." Duncan inclined his head toward me, then used the dropper to extract liquid and spread a line of it on the wall.

An eyeshadow brush would have worked better, assuming it

didn't disintegrate, but maybe Abrams kept himself to a minimal makeup regimen and didn't store such things in his lab.

Duncan had made a circle using about half the liquid when he frowned down at the dropper. "Oh, hell."

He showed it to me. The acid had eaten through the end of the tool.

I backed up.

"Hydrofluoric acid may be the *main* ingredient," he said.

"I think *magic* is the main ingredient." I wondered what impervious material the vial was made from.

"Either way, I'm doing my best not to touch the stuff with my finger or any other body parts." Holding the dropper and vial at arm's length, Duncan backed to the counter. He tossed the remains of the implement into a sink and delved into the drawer again.

"Yes," I said. "I assume it can also eat through skin."

"Even without magic, some acids can go right through tissues and decalcify bones. I…" He trailed off, his nose wrinkling.

Though the ventilation fan continued to run, sucking most noticeable odors out of the room, I did smell a faint acrid scent. And was that smoke drifting up from the wall?

The metal looked more like a panel rather than inches of solid steel. That was promising.

"It's working." I pointed at the smoke but worried about the intensified clinks and *tinks* coming from the door. It sounded like the bugs were trying to create their own hole to go through.

"Ah, delightful."

"There will probably be insulation in the wall and another panel," I warned.

"No problem." Duncan held up a fresh dropper that he'd found. "I've got more acid."

After carefully levering out the circular piece he'd made in the wall, he leaned in to rip out chunks of insulation. There was indeed an inner panel behind it.

I paced as he applied acid to it but halted when I noticed vapor wafting in through a crack under the door.

"Those bugs really want to knock us out." I rubbed my still-numb fingertips together.

Duncan glanced that way. "The vapor might do more than that."

"Comforting."

"I'll fling the rest of this acid at them if they force their way in."

"I'm getting my money's worth for Rue's services."

"How much did she charge for this?" Duncan held up the almost depleted vial.

"It was a free sample."

"Oh? That's always an excellent way to sell product."

"No doubt she expects I want to order a five-gallon vat."

"Do you have rules against making such concoctions in your apartment complex?" Duncan put the cap back on the vial and backed away from the wall. He'd finished applying the acid to the inner panel.

"It's in the lease that you can't grow psychedelic mushrooms or marijuana. Oddly, the mixing of toxic chemicals isn't mentioned."

"Might be time to make an amendment." Duncan lifted his foot and slammed his heel into the panel.

The second piece he'd created indented a couple of inches, but he wobbled, almost losing his balance as he brought his leg down. I rushed forward to keep him from pitching sideways.

"I don't need help," he snapped with irritation. Or maybe *indignation.*

But he did. I gripped his arm to keep him steady—and on his feet.

His shoulders slumped. "I *do* need help. And I hate it."

"I know. It's hard being weak when you've always been powerful."

"It's hard being weak, period."

"Some people have more experience with it and can compensate."

"And those without experience just get cranky?" He smiled ruefully.

"I think so." Gently, I pushed him to the side.

Trying not to look at the gaseous substance flowing under the door and into the laboratory, I took the second kick myself. The circle in the panel resisted flying free. Was there something blocking the wall? Maybe it needed a little more acid.

"At least the fan is sucking those vapors away." Duncan pointed at the cloud flowing under the door and immediately wafting toward the vent.

After donning gloves, I took the vial and smeared the last of the acid onto the panel.

"Not enough left to fling at metal bugs." I tossed the empty vial onto a countertop.

"Alas. You should have ordered the five-gallon vat."

"I can only imagine what Rue would charge for that."

Once more, I kicked the inner panel. It barely gave, the acid not having had time to fully work, but it did shift outward an inch.

A creak came from the door to the room, then the door fell open. I gaped. Had the bugs done that? The entire door hit the floor.

"They destroyed the hinges," Duncan said as metal bugs flowed into the room, all with their orifices open, all spewing out the hazy vapor.

"Industrious bastards, aren't they?" I kicked again.

The panel flew away and into the dark room beyond.

I scrambled through the hole, then reached back for Duncan.

As soon as he came through after me, I patted around on the floor, found the section of panel, and did my best to plug up the hole.

In the dark, I had no idea what kind of room we entered, but I doubted it was another laboratory with a ventilation fan. If the vapor-spewing bugs made it in here, we would be screwed.

22

WITH OUR BACKS TO THE PLUGGED HOLE IN THE WALL, WE SHONE our phones' flashlights around a room smaller than the laboratory we'd left. Built-in shelves and cabinets held all manner of items from jars and vials to decorations from around the world, everything from shrunken heads to glowing geodes to strange fossils. It was only luck that we hadn't been blocked from entering by some of those cabinets.

Books filled a few cases in the back, old tomes with yellowed pages. Maps and diagrams, many framed and some with notes scribbled on them, lined the walls. A few desks, chairs, and a table occupied the floor space.

I stared at the table. Numerous magical artifacts rested on it, a leather-bound journal open next to them, fresh ink on the pages. I recognized a platter and a pistol. Radomir had made me touch them when I'd been in his office at the lavender farm. And was that... Ivan's bracelet? Like the other artifacts, it emanated magic. Since I knew who that belonged to, I tucked it into my bag so I could return it later.

"This is Abrams's workspace," Duncan said, though I would

have guessed that on my own. "I recognize some of this stuff. He had it when I was a kid." Duncan waved toward some of the knickknacks on the shelves. "I'm surprised he salvaged it after..."

"After you burned his castle down?"

"Yeah."

I walked to the journal, wondering if we would be able to read the language it was written in. It looked like English, but the cursive script was tiny and jammed together.

"It wasn't a malevolent burning," Duncan said.

"I know you were trying to escape. And still lament the loss of the library."

"That's the truth. There were so many wondrous tales in there." He joined me at the table, resting his hands on it and leaning his weight on them.

"I hope your collapse isn't imminent," I told him.

"You won't carry me out if it is?"

"Oh, I will, but it'll be hard with guardian bugs nipping at my heels."

Scrapes and *tinks* came not only from the room we'd left but the door leading back out to the main area. I tried not to think about how we might be trapped.

"I have no doubt." Duncan pointed at the journal. "That's Abrams's writing."

"Can you read it?" I asked.

"It's in English."

"That looks like the chicken-scratch font. Except a lot less legible."

"It's not the finest penmanship."

"No kidding."

Maybe Duncan had grown up reading the stuff because he perused it without apparent trouble. Taking pity on me, he read aloud.

"Most of the werewolf artifacts we've discovered have yielded few clues about the magic inherent in their kind. Many were crafted by druids rather than those with lycanthropic blood. One exception is the Medallion of Memory and Power, two of which we've recently discovered, having belonged to a werewolf pack originally from the Mediterranean region where the magic of their kind was known to be strong. The werewolves themselves, many generations removed from their more potent ancestors, lack substantial magical power, but, as our silver bullets have proven, they do retain the regenerative magic that we seek to capture. It is not presently known if they possess atypical longevity, but my work on that has progressed well even without lupine influence. Based on our ingredients and my research, and touched by the magic of the medallion, my potions may achieve all that we've desired, an elixir that not only causes rapid healing and mitochondrial repair but that extends the life of the imbiber, perhaps indefinitely. Radomir may get his wish, to cash in on being able to sell eternal life to those who can afford it. I only seek to leave behind a suitable legacy and to ensure that those worthy of great longevity have a way to possess it. I'm very close now to locking in that goal. The magic of that medallion is all that I need. I am certain of it. Though the intriguing druidic case may also hold clues. As soon as I have these items, I should be able to successfully complete my life's work."

Duncan leaned back. "I figured it was something like that."

"That he's trying to create longevity potions?"

"I knew he was intrigued by the regenerative abilities of our kind and trying to bottle that power for humans, as it were. Back when I was a boy, he asked me to bite him. He wanted to be turned into a werewolf so he could easily take blood samples of one to study. In those days, he never mentioned *what* he wanted to achieve or study, so I could only guess. But a few words I've overheard since he's come back into my life... Well, this makes sense." Duncan waved at the journal. "I know that he once believed our blood was key in figuring things out. Maybe he studied it for a long time before shifting to this, trying to find secrets in magical artifacts."

"You didn't bite him, did you?" I would have sensed it if Abrams were a werewolf.

"I refused. I always thought it was a trap or a test, that he wanted me to try and would use it as an excuse to punish me." Voice low, Duncan added, "He was always quick to punish me." He flexed one of his hands, the scar tissue around his wrist visible below the edge of his sleeve. "In fact, it was shortly after we argued about that that I made my escape."

"Do you think he *still* wants to be turned into a werewolf?" I almost pointed out that there were plenty of our kind around that he could have asked to bite him, but only those who could turn into a bipedfuris had the power to pass along lycanthropy that way.

"I don't know. It doesn't, as he pointed out, convey longevity. That may be why, however, that he had Lykos made. I don't think the kid is yet old enough to pass along lycanthropy, as that ability, I believe, comes with puberty." Duncan shrugged, looking toward the door and the wall, the sounds of the guard bugs still audible. "If he's moved from wanting werewolf blood for his experiments to wanting artifacts, he may be past desiring to turn into one himself."

"If we could find some samples of what he's been working on, do you think they could cure you of your problem?" I waved toward the scar on his forehead.

A longevity potion ought to keep someone from dying because of a curse, right?

"It doesn't sound like he's cracked the code yet. Even if he had, which of those hundreds of vials in the fridge would I quaff? I didn't see labels." Louder scratches near the plug in the wall made Duncan look in that direction. "It might also be difficult to reach those fridges at the moment. Due to the bug infestation this building is suffering from."

I huffed a frustrated breath and started opening drawers and cabinets. There had to be an immediate answer to *Duncan's* problem here. If there wasn't...

I shook my head, throat tight, well aware of how quickly he was deteriorating. We didn't have time for Abrams to make a scientific breakthrough, damn it. We needed an answer *now*.

The door fell away with a clang, and bugs rushed inside, tinking, clinking, and oozing clouds of that vapor into the air. Shit.

"Time to go," Duncan said.

He ran around the table but clipped his hip on the corner. That shouldn't have fazed him, but he pitched forward, legs wobbly as several bugs sailed toward him, spewing vapor into the air more rapidly than before. It hazed the whole room.

My heart beat erratically, and numbness spread from my fingers into my arms and legs. Duncan covered his nose and mouth with his arm and kicked one of the approaching bugs. It flew into the wall but not before spitting an electrical charge into the air. It must have struck Duncan when he contacted it, because he stumbled back. More bugs swarmed closer.

Furious, I rushed to grab him. But with my legs growing more numb by the second, I almost fell too. Frustration and fear swept through my veins, and my skin pricked with hot magic. The power of the moon flowed into me, and all I managed to fling aside was my bag before fur started sprouting from my skin. I also thrust my grenade at Duncan before the wolf overtook me.

Dropping to all fours didn't make the bugs any less daunting, not with those vapors flooding my nostrils and their red glowing eyes even closer to mine. Though the wolf magic didn't eradicate the numbness creeping into my body, I sprang for the door, trying to scatter the mechanical obstacles as I rushed through them.

A memory percolated through my lupine thoughts. Duncan,

the one I wished to be my mate, was ill and couldn't change. I had to clear the way for him.

Electric shocks assaulted me whenever I touched one of the strange contraptions, but I accepted the pain, biting into the metal things and hurling them aside. I wanted to destroy them utterly, but their carapaces were strong, deterring even my magically enhanced jaws.

Some I batted with my paws, sending them skidding away, but I dared not delay long. Awareness that something in my blood was slowing me down, something that might knock me out or kill me, forced me toward the door. Instinct urged me to go as quickly as possible, to reach fresh, natural air.

But more bugs flooded in from the larger room outside of this one, piling atop each other and blocking the exit. Worse, the poison clouding the air grew thicker and thicker. I stumbled, almost pitching to my shoulder.

"Luna," came a raspy voice from behind, followed by a thump. "This way."

Duncan had grabbed my bag, slung it over his shoulder, and unplugged a hole in the wall. He waved for me to follow him, then crawled through.

Weren't there more of those bugs in the other part of this cave? I thought so, but the air in here was so toxic, sweet and cloying and deadly. Perhaps it would be better over there. Even if it wasn't, I had to go with Duncan.

He almost fell through to the other side. With more bugs piling through the doorway and surging toward me, the poisoned air crackling with electricity, I leaped through the hole. I landed beside Duncan. From one knee, he pointed past the laboratory counters and to the doorway. A handful of bugs were inside with us, but most had gone into the other room. Others were... they were clumped together and appeared to be stuck to a dark cylinder on the floor, legs and carapaces caught by its pull. Its *magnetic* pull. Duncan must have hurled one of his fishing tools ahead of him into the room.

"Hurry," he said, then lifted a paw-sized oblong metal object. "I've got this for the others. I'll follow right behind."

What it was eluded my wolf brain, but Duncan was a strong bipedfuris when he wasn't ill, and my instincts instructed me to follow his guidance. I ran out the doorway and toward the scent of pine trees and snow that wafted down from a stairwell. Escape lay in that direction.

Duncan stumbled after me, and I made myself slow, offering my back if he needed to rest a hand on it for support.

"That way." He pointed at the stairs. "Go."

The bugs in the room we'd left had realized we'd departed and were flowing out the doorway after us. Duncan pulled a slender piece out of the metal object, then rolled the device toward them. He turned to run toward the stairs, but his legs almost betrayed him. Again, he stumbled.

Despite his order, I drew close to him, again offering my back. This time, he rested his hand and some of his weight on me. Together we hurried toward the stairs.

We'd only made it up two steps when a great explosion ripped through the air behind us.

The stairs trembled, and the walls quaked. Duncan stumbled but grunted with determination and kept going, fingers digging into my fur as we climbed. He needed my support.

I gave it, but fear and instinct made me want to sprint up and outside, especially when the stairs continued quaking. Snaps and cracks came from the structure all around us. Worse, the memory of bars blocking the exit wafted through my mind. It wouldn't be easy to escape out into the forest.

We climbed as fast as we could and had almost reached the level above, that which led to the outdoors, when something snapped right over our heads.

Before I knew what was happening, the roof of the cave gave way. As it collapsed, Duncan sprang atop me, protectively pushing his body over mine. I wanted to object, since he was far weaker than I in that moment, but great chunks of heavy gray rock pummeled us. Duncan covered my head as the cave roof collapsed atop us.

23

So much weight crushed me that I struggled to move, even to breathe. Above me, Duncan groaned, his body pressed atop mine, his arms covering my head. To the sides, nothing but jagged rock poked into my flanks. The air still smelled sweet and foul, the taint of poison coating my mouth along with the dust from the fallen rubble.

As all the rock settled, it grew silent. The *tinks* of those strange metal constructs had faded. I hoped they had been destroyed by this rockfall.

Duncan groaned again and shifted, trying to push away from me, to shove the rock off us. But his muscles shook and lacked the strength for the effort. Too much weight smothered us.

I was able to turn my head enough to lick his jaw, to let him know that I appreciated the effort.

"Oh, Luna," he rasped. "I meant for you to get away. I was going to stay behind and make sure the bugs didn't kill you. I didn't mean—" Coughs broke up his words. "I didn't mean for us *both* to be trapped."

I tried to shift, thinking I might have the strength to move the rocks, but that poison had sapped me of strength as well. More, it threatened to stop my heart. In the stillness under the rock pile, I could feel its beats, rapid and strained.

Somewhere in the distance, beyond the remaining walls of this structure, a faint rumble reached my ears. The noise from a human vehicle?

Duncan must have heard it because he growled. "I have one more grenade. If that's Abrams or Radomir... maybe I can take them down with us. I'd rather you survive though. Damn it, Luna." He snarled and heaved again, pouring the last of his energy into the effort.

A few clunks sounded. Rocks shifting and falling off our pile? I also tried to thrust upward.

As we combined forces, straining together, magic flared, startling a yip from me. It had been pitch dark under the rockfall, but a glow came from somewhere. Duncan's chest. The medallion he wore.

It emanated powerful werewolf magic, and I remembered him using it in our last battle. Could it help us again now? Maybe it could fling the rocks aside.

The light and magic from the medallion flowed into Duncan. Some of it crept into me as well, and I felt it zinging through my veins. It rejuvenated me, and my paws tingled, almost hurting, as if they were waking up after falling asleep under my weight.

Duncan's aura rippled. Was he shifting? When he'd said he couldn't? The magic of the medallion had to be rejuvenating him too, giving him strength.

Something clunked softly onto the rubble next to me. One of the oblong objects? He'd released it. Alarm blasted through me. Would it cause another explosion?

No hint of tension tightened Duncan's body. Instead, his power fluctuated, and he shifted, turning not into a wolf but the bipedfuris, his torso and limbs growing thick and strong with layers of muscle. This time, when he flexed and heaved, rocks went flying, clattering against whatever walls remained around us.

A hint of fresh air reached my nostrils. I gulped it in eagerly and also pushed, the weight lessening, thanks to Duncan's efforts.

Rocks shifted away from me, and I sprang out of the rubble pile. I landed on all fours in a hallway, the floor cracked and buckled. The bipedfuris also sloughed off rubble and leaped out of the pile.

The explosive hadn't detonated. He must simply have let go of it so that he could shift without losing it.

A clattering came from one end of the hallway, bars across a doorway rising. Numerous men stood on the other side, all pointing rifles in my direction.

Duncan grasped the oblong object. Claws scraping at it, he pulled a slender stick from it. As the men at the end of the hallway stepped into the building, rifles raised as they squinted into the gloom, he hurled the object toward them.

It clattered and bounced off the wall and floor, then skidded in their direction. They cursed and ran outside.

Duncan patted my back, then led me in the opposite direction, toward another door. Another way out, I hoped.

The poison lingered in my body, making my limbs leaden, but I kept pace with Duncan, even outpacing him, four legs always faster than two.

One of the mechanical bugs blocked the way. Alone, it did little to intimidate. I sprang upon it and bit down, accepting a jolt of electricity to my jaws, and flung it away. It crashed into a wall and did not pursue us.

We rushed into a cavernous room as an explosion ripped behind us. Someone cried out, but I believed the men had backed away soon enough to avoid being blown up. Too bad. They had been sent by our enemies, I had no doubt.

The bipedfuris raced toward a metal door, but bars had

descended in front of it and remained down. He grasped them and attempted to break them. Though his muscles strained with great power, he hadn't yet regained all of his strength. He snarled and heaved, but the bars remained in place.

Another wall held giant doors meant for human vehicles. Though such things mattered little to a wolf, I'd seen similar doors numerous times. I remembered that buttons could move them. Was one such button mounted on the wall by the door we'd just exited?

As I contemplated the spot, gunshots rang out from the far end of the hallway. Whatever damage the explosion had caused hadn't been enough to stop those men, and they were charging into the building with their firearms.

I barked to alert Duncan to the button. With hands closer to what humans had than my paws, he could more easily press it. But his back was to me as he continued to try to rip away those bars.

Men ran down the hall, someone yelling, "Are you sure it's safe?"

I jumped up, attempting to press the button with my nose. It took three tries, my leaden muscles struggling to lift me, but the rumble of a motor finally sounded.

As one of the giant doors rolled up, Duncan whirled away from the bars. Together, we ran for the exit, my lungs gratefully sucking in fresh air.

The ground and walls shuddered, however, as if the opening of the door had removed a support that the damaged building needed. Or maybe the operation of the motor had shaken something loose.

I did not care why it happened, knowing only that, as we sprinted outside, a beam and wall fell behind us. Men cursed as pieces of the structure collapsed on top of them.

There were more men in the walled yard outside. Duncan ran

straight toward them, springing upon them before they could shoot.

The gate we'd climbed earlier stood open. A familiar armored vehicle idled out there, an older man in a suit standing beside it. He was pointing not at us but at Duncan's rolling den. Its doors were all open, bulky men tearing out equipment as they searched for who knew what.

Realizing the older man in charge was one of our key enemies, I ran toward him.

Duncan must have also spotted him—or maybe the defiling of his rolling den—because he roared with indignation. He also raced toward the gate.

The older man—Radomir was his name, I remembered—heard that roar and whirled toward us. He withdrew a handgun from a pocket. Duncan rushed not toward him but toward the van, springing upon those tearing its innards out.

More focused on my enemy—the most *important* enemy—I sprang over the hood of the armored vehicle. Seeing my snarling visage and my deadly fangs must have worried the man because he fumbled the handgun. Instead of firing, he ducked.

I managed to clip him as I sailed over, biting for his head. All I got was the tip of his ear, but blood spattered, and he screamed.

My momentum carried me several feet past him. When I landed, I whirled, intending to spring. He flung himself into the driver's seat of the vehicle. Though I didn't hesitate to leap, his fear made him fast, and he slammed the door shut before I reached him. Instead, I hit the hard metal side of the vehicle, bounced off, and rolled away.

Tires crunched on gravel as the engine roared.

I jumped to my paws. The vehicle turned toward me, and I crouched to spring away.

A great furred-and-fanged being leaped into view, landing on the roof of the vehicle. The bipedfuris. Men lay dead around the van, weapons scattered and useless, blood seeping into the gravel.

In the vehicle, Radomir accelerated.

I skittered to the side, evading it and ducking between two trees for cover. Radomir glared out the window at me, and I knew he'd wanted to crush me, to roll over my body and kill me. I snarled, but he didn't see it. Right atop him, crouched on the roof, Duncan raked his claws into the frame of the armored vehicle.

Radomir sped up, no doubt hoping a tree branch would knock him off, as it had once before.

Worried the old man would prove wily and get the best of even a powerful bipedfuris, I rushed down the road after them. I leaped and landed atop the vehicle, my claws scrabbling for purchase on the slick roof.

With his human-like hands and fingers, the bipedfuris had an easier time remaining secure on the moving vehicle. As Radomir drove, Duncan kept smashing and clawing the frame, trying to find a weakness in its armor. The windshield cracked under his assault.

"I thought that was bulletproof!" someone inside yelled.

"It's not *wolf*-proof."

"Go faster!"

Radomir turned the vehicle left and right, its movements jerky. He was trying to fling us off.

A window on the side opposite Radomir must have rolled down because a younger man rose into view. Half hanging out the side of the vehicle, he one-handedly lifted a rifle above the roof. He glanced at me but pointed it at Duncan.

Focused on Radomir, roaring and trying to reach him, Duncan didn't seem to see the new threat.

Though my paws slipped on the metal, the perch made even more precarious by the wild driving, I lunged toward the gunman. Just before he fired, I knocked my snout into the rifle. The barrel jerked upward, and the bullet sped into the night. It left a silver blaze, a reminder that the magical ammunition could harm or *kill* a werewolf.

Yelling, the man tried to club me with the rifle. Despite my dubious perch, I managed to catch it out of the air, wrapping my jaws around it. I tore it from the man's grip and flung it into the trees, then I bit his arm and pulled. He screamed and tried to yank away, but I had the strength to sink low and keep my fangs wrapped around his limb. I wouldn't release him so that he could draw out another weapon with which to attack us.

A wind swept across the roof, startling me. The trees to the sides had disappeared, and the vehicle was driving onto a narrow road that followed a cliff, a stream visible far below.

The man I gripped pushed farther out of his seat so that he could bring his other arm out. He attempted to punch me, his face contorted in pain from my bite. His awkward position made his blow ineffective, and I not only sank my fangs in deeper but pulled. Fear flashed in his eyes as I yanked him through the window.

He tumbled out, landing on the road, one of the tires almost rolling over him. A great shattering of glass sounded.

I looked in time to see the bipedfuris reach through a gaping hole in the windshield and rip out... a piece of the vehicle. A circle attached to a shaft with broken wires dangling from it. He pitched it into the ravine as the driver—Radomir—screamed.

There was a bend in the road ahead. If the vehicle didn't turn to follow it, we would smash into the rock wall.

I barked a warning and leaped off the roof, assuming Duncan would do the same. But he reached through the windshield. Trying to pull out Radomir?

I barked another warning. Duncan glanced around and saw the danger. He crouched to spring off the roof of the vehicle before impact, but something long and metal thrust through the broken windshield. It startled him and must have hurt because his face contorted with pain.

He kicked at the object that had attacked him, a bladed weapon Radomir had grabbed, but the vehicle hit the rock wall, and Duncan lost his balance. After smashing into the cliff, it bounced toward the ravine and over the edge. Duncan twisted and jumped as it fell, but he couldn't reach safety.

Horrified, I stared as the vehicle and Duncan disappeared from my view. Fear gripped me, and I couldn't move for several seconds. Not until a thunderous crash sounded far below. The vehicle landing.

Dread walked with me as I padded to the edge of the cliff and peered over.

The armored vehicle had stood up to bipedfuris claws, but even it hadn't been able to endure the fall. It lay smashed at the bottom, Radomir thrown out, the lower half of his mangled body sprawled in the stream.

And Duncan?

He lay on the far side of the waterway, not moving.

24

THE WOLF MAGIC DIDN'T LEAVE ME UNTIL I FOUND A WAY TO THE bottom of the cliff, the scent of the stream and burning leather and heated metal guiding me toward the wreck. As soon as it did, leaving me a naked human woman in a dark forest, I struggled to find my way with dulled senses. The tears leaking from my eyes would have made it hard to see even if there had been more light. At least the night was still and quiet, and I could hear the gurgle of water.

I patted my way through the trees, hoping that Duncan had somehow survived that fall. As a bipedfuris, he had great stamina and strength, not to mention the regenerative ability of were-wolves. But he'd been dying before all this started, weakened by that damn curse.

The tears blinded me, and I dashed them angrily away. If Duncan was alive, he would need me to keep my shit together, to call for an ambulance.

"That would be easier if I hadn't lost my clothes." And my phone? That might have disappeared too. I hadn't thought to throw it clear before I'd changed. Even if I had, it would have been buried under rubble by now.

I stubbed my toe on a rock. Frustrated, I howled. In this form, it sounded more like a maniacal scream. I didn't care. I was so tired of having these enemies and of everyone I cared about being threatened. Duncan might be dead, and this hadn't even been his battle. Radomir hadn't ever cared about him, other than wanting to use him. He and Abrams had been after my family's artifacts.

Duncan had risked his life—no, he might have *given* his life—for me.

Ahead, a magical glow made me pause. Was that... the medallion?

I remembered how it had started glowing in the building, its magic helping Duncan, helping both of us escape from the rubble.

Not caring about stubbed toes, I hurried forward, hope propelling me.

When I came out of the trees by the stream, I almost stepped on Radomir. He and the mangled SUV were on the same side of the waterway as I was. No, he was still half in it. He must have died upon impact. His eyes were frozen open, his spine twisted at an impossible angle. I couldn't summon any sympathy for the bastard.

I jumped across the stream, wincing at a rock under my bare sole, and scrambled through grass and leaves toward Duncan. His wolf magic had also left him, and he lay on his back as a naked human, but the medallion remained active. Its glow wrapped around him, the air buzzing with its energy.

Surely, it wouldn't do that if he were dead?

As I crept into the influence of the light, I hoped it wouldn't object to my presence. My mom's medallion had never zapped me or pushed me away, but who knew what this one would do?

Its glow was warm, however, and inviting. It spread over my skin like spring sun, pleasant and welcoming. The magic drew me closer to Duncan, and, in the light, the rise and fall of his chest was visible.

"Thank the moon." I dropped to my knees beside him and rested my hand on his chest.

Magic beamed up from the medallion, enveloping us both. As I had a couple of times before with these artifacts, I sensed a touch of emotion from it. Satisfaction? Over us defeating one of our enemies? No, I decided. This was about... Oh, that was it. Duncan had proven himself.

By defending me? One of the Snohomish Savagers? Or just by being willing to risk his life and give everything to fight an enemy?

I didn't know, and the medallion didn't say, but its energy continued to bathe us both for long moments. It soothed, or maybe it *healed* the wounds I'd received during the night's battles.

Finally, Duncan stirred under my hand. His head turned toward me as his eyes opened.

Relieved, I smiled, though more tears also came to my eyes. Tears of relief, this time. I wiped them away and tried to keep the smile on my face for him.

"My lady," he whispered. "Are your lips twitching?"

"Yeah, probably so."

"Ah, lovely." He puckered his.

I laughed and kissed him. We were both too weary for it to turn into anything heated, and Duncan paused to point toward the wrecked SUV. "You'll be delighted to know that he stabbed me with something familiar."

"Oh?" I asked.

Duncan lifted his naked leg, showing a puncture wound, though it already appeared to be healing. Because of his regenerative abilities or because the medallion was taking care of him? Maybe some of both.

"Radomir had your sword."

"Oh, is *that* what he stabbed you with?"

"I would have been alarmed if it had been anything else."

"I would think a sword would also be alarming."

"I suppose that's true. But if we search a bit, we should be able to find it in the wreckage. Then coming up here won't have been a waste of time."

We'd defeated one of the enemies who'd been vexing us all winter. I didn't think this had been a waste and meant to say so, but the light of the medallion brightened again. I pulled back, eyeing it warily. It beamed upward, flowing around Duncan's head.

"What..." I started to ask, but the light faded again.

"I feel like someone dropped me into one of those tanning beds." Duncan lifted a hand to his face, as if checking for a sunburn, but his fingers drifted to his forehead.

My lips parted in surprise.

"The scar is gone," I blurted.

"Gone?" Duncan probed the area in wonder. "I've had it my whole life."

"Your forehead is smooth now. The medallion..."

"I think... Yes, I'm quite sure, since I'm feeling rather good for a man who pitched off a cliff, that it lifted the curse." He nodded with certainty.

"It found you worthy."

"That's a relief." This time, *his* lips twitched.

"I should think so."

Duncan pushed himself into a sitting position and wrapped his arms around me. At the bottom of a ravine, with the wreck smoldering behind us, we finally kissed each other without interruption.

EPILOGUE

Dawn came and went, and Duncan barely stirred on my couch.

After climbing out of the ravine, putting his pillaged van back in order, and finding clothes to wear, we'd had to hunt all over to locate his keys and my phone. We'd been lucky they hadn't disappeared into the ether during our unplanned changes. For a while, I'd thought they had. Between the explosions, the partial collapse of the building, and the dead bodies that the bipedfuris had left behind, it had been a difficult and gruesome scene to search. At least, that far into the wilderness, nobody had reported the noise to the police, so we'd been able to poke around undisturbed.

Well after midnight, we'd driven home and finally arrived at Sylvan Serenity. After a quick bite to eat, we'd both passed out. I would have offered Duncan a spot in my bed, but he hadn't asked, simply collapsing on the couch, unconscious before he fully settled.

This morning, he lay in the exact same position. I might have worried about him, but his aura was stronger to my senses than it had been before the medallion's healing—than it had been in more than a week. Besides, he'd fallen asleep with his head scrunched sideways against the armrest, resulting in snoring. I believed them to be the hearty snores of someone who wasn't dying.

Once he recovered, maybe we could engage in some of the activities he'd suggested—innuendoed—when he'd been dying.

The thought left me feeling optimistic as I fired up my espresso machine. I had little doubt that numerous troubles remained that would plague me—even if Radomir was dead, Abrams might prove the vengeful sort—but we'd found the sword, and we'd healed Duncan of his malady. Correction: he'd proven himself to the medallion, and *it* had healed him.

I almost laughed at the realization that we might not have needed to go up there and endure all that. Maybe he could have gotten into a bar fight to prove he was worthy to be an alpha. No, probably not. Whatever sentience guided these artifacts was smarter than that. Besides, we wouldn't have found the sword in a bar.

Leaving it on the floor next to the couch for Duncan to sleep-guard, I took a latte and stepped outside, intending to head to the leasing office to catch up on work. A recently marked rhododendron in front of my apartment made me pause, my nose keen enough to pick up a scent that hadn't been left by one of the tenant's dogs. A *wolf* had been by. One I'd met before.

Izzy.

I sighed, certain she'd peed on the bush to leave a message specifically for me. I stepped back into my apartment and grabbed the bracelet we'd found in Abrams's underground office. Since it was magical, it had been easier to locate than my phone. If I sent it back to Ivan, would his sister leave me alone?

"Let's hope," I muttered, though I had a feeling I would see her again.

In the leasing office, I poked through drawers until I found a box suitable for shipping the bracelet. If I delivered it in person, Ivan might hit on me, and I wasn't in the mood for that.

Bolin arrived while I was addressing the box.

"I've got good news for you, Luna," he said.

"Good news? For me? I didn't know such a thing existed."

"It's about our putative buyers."

"Oh?" I asked warily.

"Yup. They pulled out, just like you thought they would. My parents think they got cold feet."

"They got cold... something."

The memory of Radomir's mangled body at the bottom of the cliff came to mind, legs dangling in the stream. Had the authorities or his minions found it yet? Did Abrams know what had happened?

"I'm glad it turned out that way," Bolin said. "*Especially* after that farce of a building inspection, I believed everything you said about them, that they weren't legitimate buyers. I tried to tell my parents, but..." He spread his arms. "They didn't want to listen. They're bummed that the deal fell through, but I'm glad."

"I suppose they'll put the listing back on the market."

Even though I was relieved Radomir wasn't in the picture any longer, nothing had changed as far as my future work and living arrangements were concerned. Another seller would come along, and I'd have to uproot my life and figure out something new.

"Yeah, sorry. I know you would prefer that things stay the same, but..."

"Is there nothing that could change their minds about selling this place? What if— Well, I can't promise anything..." Especially not with Abrams still out there. "Still, what if weird things stopped happening here? That was what prompted them to want to sell in the first place, wasn't it? The increased crime and, uh, paranormal activity in Shoreline?"

"I think it's what put the idea in their minds, yeah."

Not sure my actions at the movie theater would ensure the local thugs didn't come around anymore, I didn't promise that, but I *hoped* I'd made my point and that things would quiet down.

"It was going to happen sooner or later anyway, though," Bolin added. "Like I told you, they've been starting to talk about retirement plans. Or at least simplifying their portfolio and handing off only the really good properties to the next generation to manage." He touched his chest. "They said they're waiting for me to be more experienced and mature but that they want me to one day run everything."

"More experienced and mature? So we've got, what, twenty years?"

"Ha ha. Do you want me to get you into any more networking events? Jasmine said she would try again. She's still job hunting."

"Oh, right. How did non-alcoholic espresso-martini night go?"

How had their *date* gone? I didn't say that.

Bolin twisted his lips. "The recipe I found basically made a thin coffee-flavored chocolate milkshake."

"Isn't that okay? Those are good flavors."

"True, but I may need to stick to alcoholic drinks when I'm—Er, I could have used a little fortification to have the necessary bravery to..." His cheeks flushed red.

"Does that mean your drink-making didn't lead to a night of amore?"

His cheeks reddened further. "The night was fine, just not as triumphant as I thought it would be."

"I don't know if that implies you lost your nerve or need a druidic potion to enhance your... twig."

"I don't need any *potions*," he whispered hoarsely and glanced around, as if hordes of tenants might be at the window listening in.

His whole face was red now, and I lifted an apologetic hand. I hadn't meant to tease or torment him.

"I got nervous. That's all." He backed to the door and gripped the knob. "You didn't answer. Do you want more invitations to networking events? There's one coming up at the yacht club."

"Thanks, but I'm going to check out one of the meetups at the pizzeria/bowling alley."

"Probably a good idea. Fewer closets there for you to get yourself into trouble in."

"Hilarious."

"I shouldn't be the only one embarrassed here."

As Bolin opened the door to leave, a text came in on my phone. Duncan had woken up.

My lady, you've left your sword lying on the floor among the dust bunnies.

I left it there for you to guard. I figured a fearsome werewolf could deal with malevolent bunnies.

While unconscious?

Haven't you told me multiple times how magnificent you are? I'm sure you can handle it.

Such arrogance you accuse me of. I'm certain I've only told you of my fit and virile vitality.

Tempted to ask Bolin if those words all meant the same thing, I glanced up to see if he remained in the area, but he'd hustled to his SUV and was shooing birds away from it. Amazing that he'd drawn up those vines from the ether but the local bluejays and robins still didn't respect his vehicle.

"Kid needs to take my advice and get something druid-appropriate." I started to text a suitably snarky reply to Duncan, but the howl of a wolf came from the greenbelt, close enough that I had no trouble hearing it in the office. "What now?" I grumbled, thinking of Izzy.

I stepped outside to see if I recognized the howler. It could have been Izzy, but it could also have been another werewolf hired by my enemies. Radomir wouldn't be a problem going forward, but who knew what resources Abrams had at his disposal? After we'd destroyed his laboratory and caused the death of his business partner, he *had* to feel vengeful.

Outside, the howl was clearer, and I started when I realized that I did recognize the voice. Not Izzy but Lykos.

Are you expecting a younger version of yourself? I texted Duncan.

I am not.

Do you think Abrams would have sent him after us? After me?

In my lupine form, I'd faced off against the boy before, and he'd decided he couldn't take me. In a few years, once he matured fully, that would change, but, for now, he shouldn't be a threat. Hell, I'd given him chocolate *and* salami in the weeks since I'd met him. He ought to like me, Abrams be damned.

"I'm going to find out," Duncan said, startling me as he walked around the corner.

"Are you going to chase him down, tackle him, and question him?"

I'd yet to hear the kid speak and had no idea if he had the capacity or not. Who knew what kind of traumatic childhood he'd endured being raised by Abrams?

"That's not the plan I've got in mind." Duncan held up a finger, jogged to his van in the parking lot, hopped inside, and reappeared a minute later with his metal detector, his magic detector, and a case of fishing magnets all gathered in his arms. He walked back to me, though he looked like he would ultimately head across the lawn and into the woods. "I'm going to practice what you suggested."

It took me a moment to guess what he meant. "Showing him how to recover rusty bicycles from the bottoms of lakes?"

We'd been talking about children during that discussion, not little clone brothers.

"That and more," Duncan said. "In case I *do* someday get the urge to be a father, I ought to practice teaching kids."

He gave me a long look over his shoulder as he walked toward the woods. A long *heated* look. Had his ordeal seriously prompted him to consider fathering children? And did he want to do it... with me?

Flustered, I called, "What are you going to do if he's here to kick your ass?"

"I would be in all kinds of trouble, but I thankfully know someone with a werewolf-slaying sword." Duncan winked and disappeared into the woods.

"I'd better sign up for more lessons," I muttered.

THE END

www.ingramcontent.com/pod-product-compliance
Lightning Source LLC
Chambersburg PA
CBHW030257200626
46816CB00002BA/676